A HOUSE WITHOUT WALLS

Praise for the UKLA Award-winning *Welcome to Nowhere*

'Humane and empathetic . . . Not only eye-opening, important and topical, but a vivid, emotionally involving, nail-biting read . . . an effective call to action' Nicolette Jones, *Sunday Times* Children's Book of the Week

'A muscular, moving, thought-provoking book' *Guardian*

'Powerful, heartbreaking and compelling' *Scotsman*

'Not only does it explain how the war in Syria began in as clear a way as I have ever heard, but [Elizabeth Laird] makes her characters lovable, loathable – and believable. They are children of war but not defined by it . . . fascinating and sing[s] with truth' Alex O'Connell, *The Times* Children's Book of the Week

'Deeply moving . . . you can always count on Elizabeth Laird to write fearlessly but with compassion and this story will give readers plenty to think about' The Bookbag

*Books by Elizabeth Laird published
by Macmillan Children's Books*

Welcome to Nowhere
Secret Friends
Song of the Dolphin Boy
Dindy and the Elephant
The Fastest Boy in the World
The Prince Who Walked with Lions
The Witching Hour
Lost Riders
Crusade
Oranges in No Man's Land
Paradise End
Secrets of the Fearless
A Little Piece of Ground
The Garbage King
Jake's Tower
Red Sky in the Morning
Kiss the Dust

A HOUSE WITHOUT WALLS

ELIZABETH LAIRD

ILLUSTRATED BY LUCY ELDRIDGE

MACMILLAN CHILDREN'S BOOKS

First published 2019 by Macmillan Children's Books
This edition published 2020 by Macmillan Children's Books
an imprint of Pan Macmillan
The Smithson, 6 Briset Street, London EC1M 5NR
Associated companies throughout the world
www.panmacmillan.com

ISBN 978-1-5098-2824-1

Text copyright © Elizabeth Laird 2019
Illustrations copyright © Lucy Eldridge 2019

The right of Elizabeth Laird and Lucy Eldridge to be identified as
the author and illustrator of this work has been asserted by them
in accordance with the Copyright, Designs and Patents Act 1988.

All rights reserved. No part of this publication may be reproduced,
stored in a retrieval system, or transmitted, in any form or by any means
(electronic, mechanical, photocopying, recording or otherwise),
without the prior written permission of the publisher.

Pan Macmillan does not have any control over, or any responsibility for,
any author or third-party websites referred to in or on this book.

1 3 5 7 9 8 6 4 2

A CIP catalogue record for this book is available from
the British Library.

Printed and bound by CPI Group (UK) Ltd, Croydon CR0 4YY

This book is sold subject to the condition that it shall not,
by way of trade or otherwise, be lent, resold, hired out,
or otherwise circulated without the publisher's prior consent
in any form of binding or cover other than that in which
it is published and without a similar condition including this
condition being imposed on the subsequent purchaser.

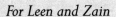
For Leen and Zain

Georgia

Turkey

Armenia

Iran

Cyprus

Syria

Lebanon

Daraa

Iraq

Israel and Palestine

Jordan

Saudi Arabia

Kuwait

CHAPTER ONE

Here are some basic facts about me:

My name is Safiya and I'm twelve years old.

I'm a Syrian from Damascus.

I'm a refugee, but I *hate* that word!

I'm a girl.

Perhaps I should also mention that my teeth stick out a bit.

So far, that's nothing special. I mean, there are loads of other people like me (maybe with nicer teeth).

So here are some slightly more interesting things you might like to know:

We had to escape in a hurry from Syria (more about that later) and came to Jordan, the country next door. That's where we live now. At least they speak Arabic in Jordan, so I didn't have to learn a new language.

I've got a twin called Saba, but I've never even met her! Well, we must have met inside our mother but we were separated when we were a few weeks old.

My mother died when we were still tiny and no one ever talked about her. She was from Jordan, actually, so it's not surprising that we ended up here. To be honest,

I never used to think much about her. How can you miss someone you never knew? Once or twice I tried to ask my Baba about her, but he always got upset, so I changed the subject. It's weird, though, because now that my life has been turned upside down I think about her all the time.

Auntie Shirin, Baba's strict older sister, came to live with us after our mother died. She was a very fussy housekeeper and scolded me all the time. 'Why don't you ever put your clothes away, Safiya?' she'd say. 'Don't you know what cupboards are for?'

I've got an older brother called Tariq who's fifteen and is very annoying. He thinks he's right about *everything*!

So here's the thing about being a Syrian girl. Boys can go where they like and do what they like, talk to anyone, walk to school on their own, meet up with friends in town. But girls have to stay at home. If I went even a little way from home on my own, my whole family would be shamed. It's just the way it is, but it doesn't mean that I like it, especially when Tariq or Auntie Shirin tell me off for silly things like not tying my hijab tightly enough, or laughing too loudly in front of other people.

And here's another thing about being a Syrian girl. You mustn't dream of ever disobeying your father. I mean *ever*. And that includes talking back to him. But no one can stop you saying things in your head! That's why I talk to myself all the time.

Saba, my twin, was taken away after we were born

because she had something blocked inside her and she needed to be rushed off to America for treatment. My uncle Hassan was going there for work, anyway, and he and his wife didn't have any children, so they offered to take Saba with them. It was their dream come true! Even when Saba was totally cured they didn't bring her back. In the end, they adopted her.

You might think it's a bit strange that Baba let his daughter go, and allowed us twins to be split up, but I think he was lost and panic-stricken after our mother died. Anyway, in Syrian families, everyone's really involved with everyone else's children, and uncles and aunties often adopt nephews and nieces.

But I don't think it was fair that no one bothered about how Saba and I would feel.

When I was very young, I never thought much about Saba. We lived in a beautiful ground-floor flat in Damascus, with a tamarind tree in the shady courtyard, marble floors and huge plummy sofas piled with cushions. There was a photo of the three of us, Tariq, Saba and me, on the china cabinet behind the dining table. Tariq was a cute three-year-old and Saba and I were tiny babies. I had my eyes open in the picture. Hers were shut and her head flopped to one side. Otherwise, we looked exactly the same. I was so used to it being there I never looked at it.

Then, when I was about seven, I started talking a lot about my twin.

'Saba's allowed to have ice cream every day,' I'd announce.

'I'm quite sure she isn't,' Auntie Shirin would reply.

'Well, anyway, she can wear her pink party dress whenever she likes,' I'd say mutinously.

Auntie Shirin wouldn't bother to answer.

An inspiration struck me one day. I'd just learned to write, and was proud of being so clever.

'I'm going to write a letter to Saba,' I told Baba as we sat eating breakfast one Saturday morning.

'That's silly,' said Tariq. 'She's American. She speaks English. You can only write in Arabic.'

'Oh.' I thought about this for a moment, then said, 'That doesn't matter. Baba can translate it into English for me.'

Baba patted my hand

'That's a lovely idea, *habibti*. I really wish you could, but your uncle seems to have changed his email address and I haven't been in touch with him for a while.'

Did he sound sad? I was too young to notice, but looking back I think he did.

I stopped talking about Saba when Farah and her family moved into the flat upstairs. Farah was in the same class as me at school, and almost at once she was the only person I wanted to be with. Saba faded out of my mind, as if she'd been an imaginary friend.

CHAPTER TWO

My father is a lawyer. In my opinion he was the best lawyer in Damascus, maybe even the whole of Syria! Being a lawyer seemed like a boring job to me when I was little – I'd wanted to be a film star, an astronaut and run an ice-cream shop all at the same time. Baba was out all day and usually came home late. Even on Fridays and Saturdays (the weekend in Syria) he'd do nothing but talk to clients on his phone, or read through piles of papers with his glasses on the end of his nose.

It slowly dawned on me that being a lawyer in Syria wasn't boring at all. In fact, it could be horribly dangerous.

Syria's my country and I'll love it forever, even if it doesn't love me, but I always knew that bad things were going on. Everyone got along fine as long as they minded their own business and never, ever, said anything bad about the government. There are secret police called the *mukhabarat*, who have eyes and ears everywhere. Sometimes it seemed as if you only had to think a rebellious thought and they'd come knocking on your door and drag you off to prison.

I think it was all that suspicion and repression that made things go so wrong. I mean, you can't keep the lid on a boiling pot forever. In the end, the steam's got to escape. And, when people did start shouting about change, the government wouldn't listen. They just tried to ram the lid down even harder on the pot. No wonder it blew off, and a full-scale civil war began.

The weird thing was that our lives went on in nearly the same old way in Damascus while the war raged elsewhere. Other places in Syria, and even the suburbs of Damascus, were being bombed to bits, but our part of town stayed more or less safe. I got used to passing burnt-out cars on my way to school, and stopped noticing the ragged holes in the front walls of some of the buildings where shells had blasted through the concrete.

I felt jumpy, though, all the time. I kept worrying that the fighting would come near us. At night I could sometimes hear explosions in the distance and I had to put my head under the blankets.

Once the war started, the *mukhabarat* were busier than ever, spying on anyone they didn't like the look of.

'You've got to be really careful, all the time,' Baba warned Tariq and me, one arm round each of our shoulders and his face unusually serious. 'Never, ever talk about politics. There are spies everywhere. Some of your teachers will be informers. Even some of your school friends.'

'I don't even know what politics is, Baba,' I protested.

He turned me to face him and took my hands in both his own.

'All right. Just remember this. Everything in Syria is perfect. We have the best government and the fairest legal system in the world.'

'But it's not true!' I objected. 'You're always saying—'

'Safiya!' Auntie Shirin said, shocked. 'Don't speak to your father like that!'

Baba let go of my hands and ran his fingers through his thick black hair. He looked desperately worried.

'You don't have to warn me, Baba,' Tariq said, trying to sound important as usual. 'If I hear people saying anything dodgy, I just walk away. We all know which teachers are the informers in my school, anyway.'

'That's just it – you don't!' said Baba earnestly. 'You really can't trust anyone, ever, outside our own immediate family. You must understand, both of you.'

'I can trust Farah,' I said.

'Not even Farah,' said Baba.

'That's—' I began indignantly.

He caught hold of my hands again.

'Listen, *habibti*, I'm a lawyer.'

'I know *that*!'

He went on as if I hadn't interrupted.

'And sometimes I have to speak up for people the government doesn't like.'

'That's good, isn't it? To make sure they're treated fairly?'

Tariq snorted.

'Fairly? In Syria?'

I ignored him.

'What it means,' Baba said carefully, 'is that the government doesn't like me much either. If the *mukhabarat* think that I sympathize with anyone – or any idea – that's critical of the government, I'll be arrested. And you know what that means.'

'Torture,' said Tariq, looking worried. 'Years in prison. No trial. Maybe even . . .'

I shivered.

Baba silenced Tariq with a look.

'There's no need to scare your sister. Nothing will happen to me if we're careful. Don't talk – ever – about anything you might see or hear at home.'

After that, it became a sort of instinct to be suspicious of everyone. The other girls at school were the same. We couldn't even say that we liked one teacher more than another in case the person we didn't like was one of *them*. No one used social media after the war really got going. It was too risky to share anything about yourself.

Sometimes a girl would come to school with red, puffy eyes and her friends would whisper, '*Her brother disappeared at a checkpoint. Her father's in prison. Her uncle's been tortured.*' After that, we'd all stay away from her, as if she had the plague. No one wanted to catch it.

CHAPTER THREE

In spite of all the worry, Farah and I still had fun together. I went up to her flat most days after school and never wanted to go home.

Farah had a sweet little baby sister, and her mother was totally different from Auntie Shirin. She was kind and untidy, and there were deep smile creases in the corners of her eyes. She was always cooking something delicious in the big warm kitchen, pushing her messy hair back from her face with the back of her floury hand.

'You're a beautiful girl, Safiya,' she said one day. 'I hope you know that.'

'I'm not,' I mumbled. 'My teeth stick out and my spots . . .'

'Oh, those things can be fixed. The main thing is that you've got a wonderful personality. You're so strong and fearless. I'm glad you're Farah's friend. You're good for her.'

And then she crushed me in a hug. I wasn't used to being hugged, and I wasn't sure if I should put my arms round her or not.

Sometimes I was so envious of Farah that I wanted to

cry. Her family made me see how much I'd missed not having a mama of my own.

Although the fighting was bad in other parts of Syria, you could still get most things in Damascus – they were just more expensive. I went with Farah and her mother one day to buy shoes. Farah wanted a pair of blue sparkly slippers. She got them, of course. Her mother could never say no. But I had Auntie Shirin's voice ringing in my ears.

'Nothing silly,' she'd said as she'd put the money into my hand. 'You need sensible black lace-ups for school that will last. I won't have you being spoiled like that Farah you're so fond of.'

I hated it when she was mean about Farah.

The next day during break I was sharing Farah's chocolate bar (she always gave me half) when a girl called Bushra saw us and came over. I groaned. Bushra was big and loud and bossy. No one liked her. For some reason, she was always getting at Farah and me. Perhaps she was jealous because we were friends.

She poked her face into mine and said, 'I saw you yesterday in the shoe shop. You and her bought the same ones, I bet. Think you're something special, don't you?'

I felt the blood rush to my head.

'We are! We're best friends!' I burst out. 'I bet you wish you had a friend, but who'd want to be friends with a bully like you?'

Then Farah started frantically pulling at my arm. She dragged me away, round the corner of the corridor.

'Are you crazy?' she hissed. 'Bushra's an informer! Her father's one of *them*!'

'You mean he's in the − in the . . . ?' I couldn't bring myself to say the dreaded word.

'Yes! Didn't you know?'

Goose bumps were running down my arms.

'Explains a lot,' I said, trying to sound brave. 'No wonder everyone's nice to her, even though she's so mean.'

I'd spoken too loudly.

'Shh!' Farah looked over her shoulder. 'Safiya, *menshan Allah*! For God's sake! Be careful!'

As we went back to our classroom, I looked up at the portrait of our president, Bashar al-Assad. That morning, like every other morning, we'd had to stand together and shout, 'We pledge our souls and our blood to save you, Bashar al-Assad!' Now his eyes seemed to follow me as I turned the corner of the corridor and bolted up the stairs. The sight of him made me shiver.

CHAPTER FOUR

The next Friday afternoon, Baba picked Tariq and me up from Koran school and took us to our favourite ice-cream shop for a treat. We'd nearly got there when he grabbed my arm and pulled me out of the way of a man coming towards us. I saw the man's eyes flicker with recognition as he passed. He gave Baba the tiniest nod and walked quickly on.

I looked back at him over my shoulder. He had a beaky nose and piercing dark eyes under low, thick eyebrows. It was the sort of face you couldn't forget.

When we got home, I said to Baba, 'Who was that man who looked like a hawk?'

'I don't know what you're talking about, *habibti*,' he said, looking irritated, and Tariq scowled at me and mouthed, *Shut up!*

There was a tense atmosphere at home after that. I would hear Auntie Shirin and Baba arguing till late at night, and whenever his phone rang Baba shut himself away in the guest sitting room by the front door so that no one could listen.

Something else was strange too. Whenever I came

home, I stumbled over a bulging holdall by the door, and my shoulder grazed a briefcase hanging from a hook above it.

'Can't we put those bags somewhere else?' I asked Auntie Shirin. 'They're in the way.'

'They're staying where they are,' she replied shortly.

One evening, I followed Tariq into his bedroom and sat down on his bed beside him.

'Something's going on, Tariq, isn't it? Do you know what it is?'

He looked at me warily.

'So you've noticed too?'

'Of course I have. What's got into Baba? He's so jumpy all the time.'

He cleared his throat. His voice had gone squeaky recently. It was worse when he was anxious.

'We shouldn't talk about it. You'll blab everything to Farah.'

'That's not fair, Tariq. I really, really won't.'

'All right, then.' He dropped his voice to a whisper as if the police might be listening even in his bedroom. 'It's one of his clients. I'm pretty sure he's in trouble with the *mukhabarat*. He—'

'I think I've seen him,' I interrupted. 'Do you remember the man who passed us in town the other day, when we were out with Baba? He looked like a hawk.'

Tariq nodded.

'That's him. He's been doing something political. It's

really dangerous. He's got Baba to do some legal work for him.'

I shuddered.

'*Wallah!* Tariq, if they arrest him, the Hawk, I mean . . .'

He nodded. I could tell he was really worried.

'They'll torture him on and on till he gives them all the names he can think of. And then they'll come for Baba too.'

I suddenly understood.

'The bags by the front door!'

'Yes. He's ready to leave at a moment's notice. To get out of the country.'

'But he can't leave us here!' I wailed. 'How would we manage without him?'

'He'll take us with him, silly. He would never leave us. I know he wouldn't.'

He reached under his bed and pulled out a backpack.

'It's packed and ready. You ought to get ready too.'

My head seemed to spin. I stared at Tariq, my stomach churning with fright.

'I'm scared,' I whispered.

He put his arm round me.

'I am too, little sister, but I'll look after you. I promise I will.'

That night, I think, I began to grow up. Farah noticed, of course. No one knew me as well as she did.

'Is something the matter?' she asked as we walked home from school the next day. 'You've gone all quiet.'

I longed to tell her everything, but I knew I mustn't.

'Got a cold coming on or something,' I mumbled.

'Come home with me, then,' she said, linking her arm through mine. 'Mama will get you something hot to eat and boil up some camomile tea.'

I hate camomile tea, but that wasn't why I pulled my arm away.

'No, I'd better get home. Don't come too close. You might catch something nasty.'

It was the only way I could warn her, but I couldn't tell if she understood.

Once at home, I went slowly to my room. The future suddenly looked scary. Surely we weren't going to leave home? What if I couldn't see Farah any more? It felt as if I was standing on the edge of a cliff and someone was about to push me over.

My foot bumped against something bulky stuffed underneath my bed. I bent down and dragged it out. A backpack! New, and full!

I began to pull everything out of it. Warm winter clothes, underwear, socks, vitamin pills. My hands started shaking.

I looked up to see Auntie Shirin standing at the door. Her face was unusually gentle as she looked at me.

'It's just in case of the worst,' she said. 'It's best to be prepared.'

'If we have to leave, you'll come too, won't you, Auntie?' I said in a wobbly voice.

She sat down on the bed beside me.

'No. I'll go and look after your grandfather. You're nearly grown up now, Safiya. You don't really need me any more.'

I understood then that I loved my Auntie Shirin. I wanted to cuddle up against her but didn't know how.

'I do need you! I do! I love you!'

Awkwardly, she patted my back.

'Come on now, *habibti*. There's no need for all this fuss. Like I said, it might never happen.'

CHAPTER FIVE

But it did happen. The very next night.

I was already in my pyjamas and I'd just said goodnight to Baba, when a thunderous knocking came at the front door.

We all froze in terror. Auntie Shirin was at the kitchen door, her hand over her mouth. Tariq had jumped up from the table, where he'd been playing a computer game. Baba, his face pale with horror, stood motionless, gripping the back of a chair.

The knocking came again.

'Safiya, Tariq, go to your rooms. Now,' said Baba.

'Baba, let me—' began Tariq.

'*Now!*' barked Baba.

I bolted like a rabbit into my bedroom. I shut the door, but left a tiny crack open so that I could watch what was happening.

Baba muttered something to Auntie Shirin then strode forward and opened the front door.

I thought I'd see stone-faced men in grey, coiled up like snakes ready to strike, who would take my Baba away. But there was only one man outside. His hand was raised to knock again, but as the door opened he almost fell in to the hallway. It was the Hawk, with his beaked nose and the eyes of a bird of prey.

He darted inside and shut the door again. His face was terribly pale.

'Adnan!' he panted. 'I'm sorry. I shouldn't have come here, but I can't trust the phone. I need those papers I left with you. Are they here?'

Auntie Shirin sank down on to a sofa shaking with shock. Baba took down the briefcase from the hook behind the door and thrust it at the Hawk, who swayed with relief.

'*Alhamdulillah*,' he said. 'Thank God.'

'What's happened?' asked Baba.

'The *mukhabarat* have got my assistant. He's loyal, but he'll tell them everything under torture. I'm getting out of the country now. Tonight.'

'Your assistant? Does he know about me?'

The Hawk shook his head.

'I don't think so. He might. Look, Adnan, I'm so sorry. I . . .'

Baba almost pushed him out of the door.

'Don't be sorry. It's been an honour to work with you. But go now.'

'What will you do?'

'We'll leave too, of course.'

'Where will you go?'

Baba actually smiled.

'Better you don't know.'

They embraced quickly, then the Hawk vanished through the front door, which Baba shut smartly behind him.

The rest of that night was a terrifying blur. I just remember standing at my bedroom door in my pink pyjamas and fluffy slippers, unable to move.

Tariq burst out of his room.

'Did I hear that right, Baba? We've got to go?'

Baba looked suddenly helpless.

'Yes. I . . .'

'When?'

'Now! Now! They could be here any minute!'

'Tonight?' Tariq's voice came out in a squeal.

Auntie Shirin had pulled herself together. She put her hand on Tariq's back and steered him to his bedroom.

'Get your things, Adnan,' she said to Baba over her shoulder. 'And you, Tariq. Come, Safiya. I'll help you.'

'But we can't go out now. It's bedtime,' I objected feebly.

No one answered.

'I wish you were coming with us,' I said as Auntie Shirin hustled me to my bedroom and into my day clothes. 'We won't be away for long, will we?'

She'd been reaching into a drawer to pull out a clean pair of socks, and she froze for a moment before she said,

'Only Allah knows what will happen. Always say your prayers, Safiya, like I taught you.'

'But where are we going?' I asked.

'Somewhere safe.'

'Where's safe?'

'Jordan. You're going to our cousins in Azraq.'

'I've never heard of Azraq.'

'It's in the east of Jordan. Yasser and Zainab are your family, Safiya. They'll look after you.'

'But who'll look after you?'

'I told you. I'm going to your grandfather. My bag is packed too. I'm going to lock up here, and go to him right away.'

Baba called out, 'Come on! Hurry!' and a moment later we were outside the house. Baba pushed me and Tariq into the back of a waiting taxi before diving into the front. Auntie Shirin ran after us and thrust our winter coats through the window.

'We don't need those. We'll be too hot,' I said, but Baba said, 'Take them, Safiya. It won't be summer forever,' and that frightened me more than anything else.

There was no time for more. The taxi sped off. The beam of the street lamp lit up the driver's face as we turned the corner. He looked terrified.

I looked back and saw that a light was on in Farah's flat.

I haven't said goodbye! I thought.

Then I realized something even worse.

'Baba, we've got to go back!' I said desperately. 'I've left my phone at home!'

Baba didn't answer, but Tariq said, 'No point. You wouldn't be able to use it, anyway. If you'd switched it on, they'd have got our location.'

'But Farah won't know where I've gone!'

Baba turned round.

'Tariq's right, *habibti*. And don't worry about Farah. She'll understand.' He was talking in an irritatingly soothing voice, as if he was speaking to a little girl.

Tariq was more brutal.

'The last thing Farah will want is to get a call from you,' he said. 'Do you want to put her family in danger?'

That was when I started crying. I tried to do it quietly, but Tariq heard. He must have felt he'd been too sharp, because he put his arm round me and tried to pull me closer.

'Hey, cheer up. I thought you always wanted to have an adventure.'

'This doesn't feel like an adventure,' I said between sniffs. 'It's more like a disaster.'

CHAPTER SIX

It was a horrible journey from Damascus to the Jordanian border. We'd been sheltered from the war in our part of the city, but as we travelled south we could see how ghastly the destruction had been. Through the taxi window I saw miles of ghostly shattered buildings and piles of rubble where houses had once stood.

There were lots of starts and stops and changes from one taxi and bus to another, and there were terrifying checkpoints where we held our breath as stone-faced men with guns leafed through our papers. The last part, as dawn was breaking, was a trek on foot across a long stretch of desert to get to the border. I was so tired that I just wanted to curl up right there on the ground and go to sleep.

The most worrying thing was that something seemed to have happened to Baba. It was like he'd broken inside. It really scared me.

We'd just crossed into Jordan and were waiting for a bus to take us to Azraq when the worst thing of all happened. Baba had pulled out his wallet to pay for our bus tickets, when someone rushed at him out of nowhere,

snatched it out of his hand and dashed off.

Baba just stood there, frozen to the spot, but Tariq yelled, 'Hey! Come back!' and sprinted after the thief. He was only a boy and Tariq nearly caught him, but another boy put out his foot and tripped Tariq up, sending him sprawling on to the rough, gritty desert ground. The two thieves disappeared, laughing, into a crowd of people.

Tariq limped back to us.

'How much was in it, Baba?' he said.

Baba was white-faced and shaking.

'All of it. All our money. And my bank card.'

The bottom dropped out of my stomach.

'What are we going to do?' I wailed.

Baba didn't answer, but Tariq, who had been just as shocked as me, put his shoulders back as if he was about to pick up a heavy load and said, 'I've got a bit of money. I think it's enough for the bus.'

But when he'd paid for the tickets we had nothing left at all. So that was how we arrived in Azraq. We'd travelled through the night and half the next day. We were exhausted, starving, desperate for a drink and a shower. And absolutely penniless.

CHAPTER SEVEN

I suppose I'd imagined that our cousin Yasser's house would be like our flat in Damascus, but it wasn't. It wasn't even in the town of Azraq itself, but on a patch of bare, stony ground about a mile away from the centre. It was painted a creamy colour and it had four rooms as well as a kitchen and bathroom. There was a breeze-block wall around a little courtyard that ran round the house. The roof wasn't finished and there were steel rods sticking up from it, ready to be used if another storey was ever built on top. There were other houses dotted about quite close by, but only one shop, a general food store, a few minutes' walk away across rough ground.

Uncle Yasser and Aunt Zainab had two children, Fares, who was eighteen and had left home to study in Amman, and Lamia, who was nine.

It must have been a shock for them when we turned up out of the blue. Uncle Yasser had written to Baba telling him that we'd be welcome to come if the war made us homeless, but I don't think he'd expected Baba to take him up on it. We called them 'Uncle' and 'Aunt' even though they were only cousins, and hardly knew Baba, after all. But family is family in the Middle East, and so they had to welcome us.

We stumbled into the house, put our bags down and then I sort of collapsed with exhaustion. Someone (I think it was Aunt Zainab) took me to a bed and I fell properly asleep. Not even an earthquake would have woken me up.

What did make me sit up at last was the smell of the most delicious food. It was dark outside. Evening already. I staggered out of the bedroom and followed my nose to the central room, where Aunt Zainab was setting out a meal on a tablecloth on the floor, in the old traditional style.

I looked around, taking everything in. This house was quite different from our old home. There were no books or pictures and not much furniture, not even a table. There was a TV, but it looked old.

The food, though, was wonderful. Lamb kebabs, aubergine stew and baby pastries with delicious fillings – the works. And Uncle Yasser had brought a big box of baklava from the bakery, little parcels of sweetness, stuffed with nuts and dripping with honey.

Maybe it was because I was so hungry, but that meal was the best I'd eaten in my whole life. I just sat there, cross-legged on a cushion, and stuffed myself.

But then, just as we were finishing, someone knocked on the metal front door, which made a horrible clanging sound.

They've followed us here! I thought. *They've come for us!*

I let out a scream and clutched at Tariq, who was sitting beside me and who had gone a funny green colour.

Aunt Zainab laughed.

'What a little rabbit you are, Safiya! Scared of a knock on the door?'

Uncle Yasser got up and frowned at her.

'It's all right,' he said kindly to me. 'Just a delivery I've been expecting.'

I went scarlet with embarrassment and let go of Tariq's arm. He was trying to smile, and Baba's hands were shaking as he picked up his glass. Lamia looked at us scornfully.

'It takes more than a knock on the door to scare *me*,' she said.

'Of course it does, darling,' said Aunt Zainab. 'Now you go off and play. Safiya will help me clear up.'

I saw how it was straight away. Aunt Zainab had waited nine years for Lamia after Fares was born. Now she was her mother's spoiled little darling. There was no chance that Aunt Zainab was going to spoil me. In fact, I could tell she didn't like me.

Maybe I wasn't easy to like? I wasn't pretty and girly, like Lamia. There's something . . . well . . . awkward about me, that doesn't exactly make me popular. I don't like it when people are mean and I tell them so. And I've got a bad temper. When something riles me, I go off like a firecracker. Anyway, Aunt Zainab resented me, right from the start.

I tried to help her, even though I didn't know what to do. We'd had a cleaner in Damascus who came in every day to mop and dust and do the laundry. Auntie Shirin didn't let me help her with the cooking or shopping either.

'Go and do your homework,' she'd say, if I ever offered to help her. 'You'll only get in my way.'

Aunt Zainab was quite different. After the first few days she started ordering me around like a servant, while Lamia looked on, smirking. Luckily, she was at school most of the time.

There was no point expecting Baba to stick up for me. He was too depressed to notice anything. He'd suddenly gone from being well-off and important to living on the charity of a cousin he didn't really know. It was as if he'd been thrown into a deep, mucky pond and didn't know how to swim.

He'll start getting better soon, I thought.

But he didn't.

CHAPTER EIGHT

Once we were in Jordan, the Syrian war seemed strangely more real than it had at home. Bomber planes sometimes roared overhead on their way to destroy Syrian cities. They made my stomach turn over.

Azraq was full of refugees. A lot of them had been sent to the huge camp outside town. It looked like a horrible place, with straight lines of bright white cabins marching across miles of dusty desert. No one ended up there if they could help it.

Not that I had much time to think about Syria and the war. Aunt Zainab was on at me all the time.

A few weeks after we'd arrived, she wanted me to do her shopping.

'And don't be lazy and go to Abu Ali's little shop across the way,' she said one morning, counting some money into my hand. 'It's not far to the proper grocer's on the main road.'

Luckily, Tariq was there.

'I don't think Baba would like Safiya going so far on her own, Aunt Zainab,' he said politely. 'I'll go with her.'

She shot him a sharp look, then nodded. She even looked a bit guilty.

'Of course! What was I thinking of? You're not a child any more, are you, Safiya? For a moment I was forgetting . . .'

Forgetting what? I thought. *That I'm not your servant?*

Tariq kicked out at loose stones as we walked down the dusty track towards the town.

'What's she doing, sending you running around the streets on your own?' he said. 'It's dangerous! Baba would be furious if he knew.'

'But he doesn't know, does he?' I answered bitterly. 'He doesn't notice anything anymore.'

'I'll look after you,' Tariq said in a superior kind of way. 'But you've always got to do what I tell you.'

Back home I'd have thought of a neat way to cut him down to size, but it was different here. I *did* need someone to look out for me. Azraq was a funny sort of in-between place. Thousands of people had flooded in from Syria, and long-distance trucks passed through all the time. A young girl on her own, walking along the main road, would stand out like a flaming torch. I'd never felt so vulnerable.

Tariq was still fuming about Aunt Zainab.

'She treats you like a slave!' he went on indignantly. 'I hated it yesterday when she made you wash the floor, then said you hadn't done it properly.'

'I didn't think anyone had noticed. Or cared,' I muttered.

'Well, I *do* care. And you know what, Safiya, it's up to you and me now to – I don't know – take charge. Baba's lost it. He's just not there any more.'

'He'll come back. He'll get better.'

I sounded more hopeful than I felt.

'He might. He might not. People don't always.'

We'd reached the main road and turned left off the track on to the stony path that ran alongside the tarmac. A convoy of military trucks rumbled past. They were so noisy that we had to stop talking. When they'd gone, Tariq said, 'And Lamia . . .'

'Don't even *talk* to me about Lamia. She's a horrible little brat!'

Tariq pretended to back away.

'Oo! Scary Safiya! You can't stand her, can you?'

'No, I can't. And you know what? It's a shame. I'd have loved to have a little sister, since I can't have my own twin. But Lamia! She makes digs all the time, about how we're so poor now, and things about Baba and you. You wouldn't believe some of the nasty things she's said.'

'I would, actually. I've heard her. You've been great, the way you haven't answered back.'

He'd grown taller than me recently, and I had to look up to see his face.

'Hey, big brother,' I said, trying not to show how pleased I was. 'This is a surprise. I thought I was beneath your notice.'

'Oh,' he said grandly. 'I see more than you think.'

We'd reached the strip of shops by now that lined the main road. I pushed open the door of the food shop.

'So what does madam want this time?' Tariq said, following me inside.

'Cucumbers and a big bunch of parsley,' I said. 'And that's for starters.'

I led the way to the vegetable section.

'*And mind it's fresh,*' I said, imitating Aunt Zainab's voice. '*The stuff they had last week . . .*'

'Shh!' Tariq interrupted, laughing at me. 'You sound too like her. Someone'll recognize her voice if you're not careful.'

We walked back in a friendly silence. Once inside, I put the shopping bags down on the kitchen table.

'Where have you been all this time?' Aunt Zainab said crossly. 'There's a huge load of washing to hang out. I can't be expected to do all the work around here.'

I shut my eyes and counted to ten.

'I'm sorry, Aunt Zainab. We went as quickly as we could.'

'You silly girl!' she said, tutting with annoyance. 'I told you to go to Abu Ali's on the corner! You never listen, do you?'

I wanted to turn round and storm out, but then I caught sight of Tariq, who was still standing at the kitchen door. He was making a face at Aunt Zainab's back and mouthing, *You never listen, do you?*

I stifled a giggle and swallowed my anger. I had an ally now and it felt as if the sun had broken through a big black cloud.

CHAPTER NINE

Baba and Uncle Yasser were as different as fire and water. Baba was brilliant with brainy things but he was hopelessly impractical. Uncle Yasser was a businessman, who had started with nothing and built himself up. He was good with his hands and liked solving technical problems.

Uncle Yasser seemed a bit awestruck by Baba at first, maybe because he hadn't had much education himself. I was afraid he might start despising Baba when he saw how helpless and depressed he'd become, but he just became kinder and more protective.

The three of us, Baba, Tariq and I, all felt bad about staying with Uncle Yasser and Aunt Zainab for so long. Baba kept worrying away at it.

'You've been too good to us, Yasser,' he'd say. 'We've been here for a month! It's hard on you and Zainab.'

'No, no, Adnan,' Uncle Yasser would answer earnestly. 'We're honoured that you came to us. *Be'izn Allah.* It's God's will.'

But as the weeks went past, his answers began to sound less sincere.

It was Baba who brought up the subject of a tent.

'I've seen them all over the place,' he said. 'There's no reason why we shouldn't move into one. Just until I get back on my feet. Honestly, Yasser, it would be better for all of us.'

It was a warm evening and they were sitting on a couple of white plastic chairs outside the front door as they talked. I was in the kitchen with Aunt Zainab and could hear every word. I could even hear the click of Uncle Yasser's worry beads as he let them slip through his fingers.

'That's a dreadful idea, Adnan!' he said. 'I won't hear of it! What would everyone say?'

I turned round and caught sight of Aunt Zainab's face. She'd been listening eagerly too.

She can't wait to get rid of us, I thought. *Uncle Yasser won't be able to stand up to her.*

I shivered at the thought of living in a tent. It was scary and embarrassing. We'd be like the poorest of the poor, down at the bottom of the heap. But, after a few moments' panic, I began to think what it would mean. I wouldn't be under Aunt Zainab's thumb any more. Our family would have our own space and I wouldn't have to share a bedroom with Lamia.

Tariq had come into the kitchen. I could see that he'd been listening too. I gave him a little nod. He went outside to join the men.

'I couldn't help hearing what you were saying, Uncle Yasser,' he said. 'I think a tent's a great idea. So does

Safiya. We'd manage fine on our own. We've, we've –' he paused, fishing around for the right thing to say – 'we've trespassed on your hospitality long enough.'

'No, no! I won't hear of it!' said Uncle Yasser, sounding upset. 'Please, let's change the subject.'

'Give it a week,' Tariq whispered to me later that evening. 'Aunt Zainab'll persuade him. You'll see.'

That night I couldn't sleep, thinking about the tent. Camping holidays had been fun in Syria. Before the war had started, Farah's family had gone to Palmyra, a beautiful, ancient city in the desert. They'd lit fires, sat out under the stars, slept in tents, then ridden on camels to the ruins as dawn turned the old stones pink. She'd shown me all the photos on her phone.

Palmyra had been blown to rubble now. It gave me an ache to think about it.

Anyway, our tent won't be a bit like those fancy tourist ones, I told myself.

CHAPTER TEN

Tariq was right. Uncle Yasser gave in about the tent exactly a week later. He felt bad about it, I could tell.

'I'll see to it all,' he assured Baba. 'I'll pitch it right next to the house in that fenced-off bit.'

'But that's where they used to keep goats,' I whispered to Tariq. 'It stinks.'

Tariq was excited at the thought of the tent. He wasn't bothered by a bit of goat poo.

'We'll clean it up,' was all he said. 'Think about it, Safiya, we'll be inside a proper fence. On our own! It's the best thing, really.'

Uncle Yasser did all the practical things himself, getting hold of the tent, putting it up and installing a water tank and a chemical toilet. He and Tariq spent a long time sweeping the ground, though it still smelt when they'd finished. While they were working, Baba went round the rough fence, checking to see how easy it would be for anyone to break through the ramshackle bits of corrugated iron, uprooted thorn bushes and plastic sheeting. The fence had been strong enough to keep goats in. He wanted to see if it would keep men out.

On the third day, when the tent was nearly ready to move into, Uncle Yasser brought in some rolled-up mats for the floor and three thin mattresses, which he laid round the edges of the tent, along with some pillows and bedding.

'And I've got some good news for you,' he said heartily. 'I've spoken to the director of the boys' school. He says he'll make room for Tariq. The new term starts next week. I'll get the uniform sorted out for him too.'

'That's wonderful, Yasser!' said Baba warmly. 'The children's education is what's been worrying me most.'

Tariq grinned delightedly, but then he caught my eye.

'What about Safiya, Uncle?' he said. 'She needs to go to school too.'

'I know. I'm sorry.' Uncle Yasser looked uncomfortable. 'We – I mean, your aunt – contacted the girls' school and they said that the Eighth Grade class is full. Maybe next year, eh, Safiya?'

It felt like a kick in the stomach. What was I going to do if I couldn't go to school? Didn't my education matter too? What sort of future would I have without it?

'Please, Uncle Yasser,' I said desperately, 'couldn't you ask them again?'

But he was already hurrying out of the tent.

I don't believe Aunt Zainab asked the school at all, I thought furiously. *She wants to keep me as her servant.*

'Baba, can't you do anything?' I pleaded.

He shook his head sadly.

'What can I do? Be patient, Safiya. You can make it up later. When the war ends and the government changes, maybe we can all go home to Syria.'

He didn't believe it, and neither did I. I ran out of the tent, swallowing tears, and bumped into Uncle Yasser, who was coming back in, carrying a big cardboard box.

'Your aunt says you can have these,' he said, 'and she said to tell you that you'll be welcome to eat with us tonight. No need to start cooking yet, eh, Safiya?'

My stomach dropped with fright. It hadn't occurred to me that I was expected to cook for us myself. I opened the box. It was full of old pots and dishes that had been stacked at the back of Aunt Zainab's cupboard.

The men went outside and I was left alone in the tent. I looked around. The canvas walls were grey and dusty. The mats were old and stained, and the mattresses had ugly rust-coloured covers on them.

Farah will be doing maths with Mrs Farida at this very moment, I thought, swallowing a lump in my throat. It was painful thinking about Farah. Had she been angry with me when I'd disappeared without sending her a goodbye message? Did she think I didn't care?

She's probably forgotten all about me, I thought. *Anyway, I expect she's got another best friend now.*

CHAPTER ELEVEN

I hardly slept a wink that first night in the tent. There were too many strange noises. The canvas creaked, cars hooted on the road nearby and voices shouted in the distance. It felt weird too, to be sleeping in the same room as Baba and Tariq.

I must have fallen asleep at last because I started dreaming. I was in the sitting room of our old flat and in the corner there was a door I'd never noticed before. I opened it and saw a girl right there in front of me. Twelve years old. Thick brown hair. Heavy eyebrows. The same middling height as me. Slim, like me.

'Saba!' I called out. 'Where have you been all this time?'

She turned and walked away without answering. A moment later, she was lost in a sort of hazy mist and I couldn't see her any more.

'Come back!' I called out. 'Don't go!'

I tried to follow her, but the door swung shut in my face. And then I woke up.

'I dreamed about Saba last night,' I said to Tariq as I poured out the tea I'd made for breakfast.

'Did you?' he asked curiously. 'What was she like?'

'Like me, of course!'

'That's what I was afraid of. Hey, don't look like that! I was joking!'

Just like me, I thought. *A person out there who's just like me. My twin! I could never lose her, like I've lost Farah. If only I could find her again! She'd be my other self. My friend for life!*

'Baba, where *is* Saba?' I asked. 'Do you still not know?'

'Yes, and Uncle Hassan!' said Tariq eagerly. 'He's got a good job, hasn't he? Can't you tell him what's happened to us? He's Mama's own brother. He'd help us.'

Baba shook his head.

'It's not that easy.'

'Why? What's not easy?' I asked.

'I don't know where he is! When they first moved to America, they were in Seattle, but then Hassan changed jobs and email addresses. He sent me his new one, but it must have been wrong, because when I wrote to him my message bounced back. I'd had a brush with the police by then and I was sure my emails were being intercepted, so I changed my own address. We lost touch.'

'Couldn't you have contacted his company?' asked Tariq.

'Yes, of course, but I was already under suspicion and Askil International is a Middle Eastern company. I didn't want to make things difficult for him.'

'But isn't it different, now we're here in Jordan?' I asked him. 'Aren't we out of reach of – *them*?'

Even the thought of the *mukhabarat* made me shudder.

'The thing is,' Baba said reluctantly, 'that we – Hassan and I – we made an agreement at the time. Your aunt Israa insisted. She – she's a very difficult woman.'

Tariq frowned.

'What do you mean, Baba? What agreement?'

'Being a lawyer in Syria has always had its dangers. You know that. Israa is much too protective of Saba. She's convinced she's delicate and can't stand any shocks. She was sure that if Saba knew that her father was in any kind of danger she'd be emotionally traumatized.'

'Sounds as if Saba's spoiled rotten,' Tariq said disapprovingly.

Baba ignored him.

'I think the real reason is that Israa's terrified of losing Saba. She thinks that if she knows about us she'll demand to come back and live with us and Israa will lose her altogether.'

Tariq laughed incredulously.

'That's a joke! Who'd want to live in this dump?'

I was still trying to understand.

'You don't – you can't mean that Saba doesn't know about us, Baba? About me? That we're twins?'

'Actually, she doesn't.' Baba was looking more and more uncomfortable. 'She thinks that Hassan and Israa are her real parents.'

'That's terrible!' I burst out. 'She has a *right* to know about me! I'm her *twin*!'

'And I'm her father,' said Baba, raising his hands despairingly. 'It's been so painful – *agonizing* – for me, the decisions I've had to make, since your mother . . . And look at the situation we're in now! How would that poor child feel, knowing that her family, her *real* family, were reduced to . . . to . . .'

And then the worst thing happened. He cried. He turned his head away from us, but I'd seen tears rolling down his cheeks. Tariq and I looked at each other, too shocked to speak.

'Saba's lost to us, then,' I said at last, and my voice came out in a wail.

'She needn't be,' Tariq said defiantly. 'Think about it. It's easy to find people nowadays. What was the name of the company Uncle Hassan works for again?

'Askil International.'

'Well then, all we have to do is contact their head office, explain the situation, ask . . .'

Baba shook his head violently, as if he was shaking off the tears.

'Weren't you listening to me, Tariq?' he said angrily. 'I made an agreement, most unwillingly, but I made it. Can't you see that if Hassan and Israa knew how – how wretched all this is, they'd want to protect Saba from us even more?'

'You think she'd be ashamed of us, Baba,' I burst out. 'But she wouldn't be! She's my twin! *I* know what she'd feel!'

Baba turned his furious face on me.

'*Menshan Allah*, Safiya! Can't you see that *I'd* be the one who'd be ashamed for my daughter to see us as we are now?'

He jumped up and ran out of the tent.

I wanted to shout after him, *She wouldn't be ashamed of us! She's me and I'm her!*

Something changed in me that day. Saba had always been there, a shadowy figure, more imagined than real. I hadn't ever wondered why we'd had no contact with her. It had been one of those facts of life that in my childish way I'd accepted without question, vaguely assuming that we'd meet one day, when she came back from America.

Anyway, I had Farah, I thought. *She was like my sister. Almost like a twin.*

But Farah had gone. And now I seemed to have lost Saba too, perhaps forever.

A red tide of revolt rose up inside me.

'You're wrong, Baba,' I muttered. 'I'm not going to let you keep us apart. I'm going to find Saba, and bring her back to our family, and no one's going to stop me!'

CHAPTER TWELVE

Aunt Zainab was nicer to us once we'd moved out. For the first week she sent Uncle Yasser over with some supper, then she let me know that it was time I stood on my own two feet. She gave me a starter stock of rice, oil, tomato puree, tea and sugar, and told me to get on with it.

The only thing I knew how to make was pasta with tomato sauce, but it was horribly difficult doing it on one little gas burner outside by the water tank where I'd made a sort of kitchen space. I had to squat on the ground because we didn't have a table, and cut up the onions on a plate with a blunt knife.

One afternoon I was washing Baba's shirts in the bucket by the water tank when I heard Lamia call my name. I groaned inside.

She pushed open the battered corrugated-iron gate, marched across the few metres of open ground and walked right into the tent. Lamia thought she was Bilqis Queen of Sheba and I was her lowly slave.

'Mama says you've got to come at once,' she said, standing there in her new flouncy dress, wrinkling her nose at the shirts waiting to be washed. 'Why don't you clean up, Safiya? This place is a mess.'

She didn't wait for an answer, but dashed off, leaving the gate open, the big white bow at the back of her head bouncing as she went.

'*Mama says you've got to come at once,*' I repeated under my breath. 'Thank you very much, *Princess* Lamia.'

I finished washing the shirts and hung them up on the washing line to dry. I wasn't going to hurry.

Our tent was at the side of the house, and when I went round the corner to the steps in the front I heard voices in the kitchen. Aunt Zainab's sister, Um Salim, had come to visit.

I was just about to knock on the door when I heard Aunt Zainab say, 'That's right. Adnan was a lawyer in Damascus. Quite successful, I think. But look at him now! You'd have thought he'd have pulled himself together for the sake of the children. Shown a bit more drive and energy. But it's always the same. People who think they're so clever fall to bits when anything practical has to be done. Yasser never passed an exam at school, but he's a successful businessman, running his own show. To be honest, I never really liked that Syrian side of Yasser's family. Thought they were somebodies, I can tell you. Adnan's sister, Shirin, she's a dried-up old stick. Looked down her nose at me.'

Underneath my hijab my scalp was prickling with fury.

'How *dare* you?' I hissed. 'Our family's worth a million of yours!'

Um Salim said something I didn't catch.

'The mother?' Aunt Zainab said. 'She was Jordanian, you know. They met when they were students. We went to the wedding in Amman. No expense spared!'

I was holding my breath, dying to hear more. No one ever talked about my mother. I'd asked Baba about her a few times, but he'd just looked sad and said, 'She was beautiful, *habibti*, like you,' and then he'd changed the subject. Auntie Shirin would only shake her head in an infuriating way and say, 'It was the will of Allah to take her. No point in thinking about it now.'

There'd been a photo of the wedding in Baba's bedroom. They both looked young and lovely. Sometimes when no one was around, I used to creep in and gaze at my mother in her long, white wedding dress.

'Hello, Mama,' I'd whisper to her. '*I wish you weren't dead.*'

Aunt Zainab and Um Salim were still talking.

'Wasn't her name Mariam?' Um Salim said. 'Awful what happened, wasn't it?'

'Well –' Aunt Zainab was moving around the kitchen, clattering pans – 'you could have seen it coming. I always thought she was a bit . . . you know . . . And that brother of hers! Hassan! So high and mighty you wouldn't believe it. Yasser thought he saw him a while ago, going into a building in Amman.'

I gasped, straining my ears to hear more.

'You'd have thought he'd have stepped in to help the

family,' Um Salim said. 'The children's own uncle!'

'You would indeed.'

I could almost see Aunt Zainab's thin lips snap shut.

'Then why doesn't he?'

'How should I know?' Aunt Zainab sounded exasperated. 'They were in America at one time. I've no idea if they've really come back or not. I gave up long ago trying to work out what goes on in that family. Anyway, for some reason it suits Adnan to land them all on us and sponge off Yasser, who's so soft he can't say no.'

My heart was pounding. Was Uncle Hassan really in Amman? Had the family moved back from America? Amman was only a few hours' drive away from Azraq! Saba might be much nearer than I'd thought! Somehow, I'd have to catch Uncle Yasser on his own and ask him to tell me more.

Someone moved towards the window. At any moment Aunt Zainab might look out and see me standing there on the step, listening. Quickly, I pushed the door open and went in.

Aunt Zainab and her sister were settled on the padded mats that lined the bare sitting-room walls, leaning back against plump embroidered cushions. I liked Um Salim. She was round and soft, while Aunt Zainab was hard with sharp, angry corners. They were so different it was hard to believe that they were sisters at all.

'Hello, dear,' said Um Salim. '*Kifek?* How are you?'

'You took your time,' said Aunt Zainab. She held out a

banknote. 'I want you to go over to Abu Ali's and get some coffee. Make sure it's fresh. I could hardly swallow what he sold me last week. You have to stand up to tradesmen. Give them an inch and they take a mile.'

I didn't trust myself to speak. I took the note and went to the door. I hadn't quite closed it when I heard Um Salim say, 'Honestly, Zainab. The poor little thing. Can't you see she needs a bit of loving? Why can't you be nice to her?'

There was a short silence.

'What she needs,' Aunt Zainab said, 'is *training*. She's never learned to do anything practical. *I* had to learn in the school of hard knocks. She's got to stand on her own two feet like I did, and the sooner she starts the better.'

'You shouldn't send her out on her own, anyway,' said Um Salim.

'Don't be ridiculous,' snapped Aunt Zainab. 'It's only to Abu Ali's.' She paused. 'Actually, I keep forgetting that she's not a child any more. Not that she's in much danger. Who would look twice at her, with those teeth and that dreadful skin?'

I was trembling as I walked across the dusty, stony stretch of ground between the house and Abu Ali's place.

Aunt Zainab's horrible voice was echoing in my head.

Who would look twice at her? Did you hear that, Saba? She's a mean old cat.

Abu Ali's shop was empty, except for the old man

himself. He was sitting behind the counter on a high
stool, peering down at a newspaper spread out on the
wooden surface, his glasses threatening to slip right off
his nose.

'*Ahlan wa sahlan, habibti*,' he said, looking up. 'What
can I do for you?' Then, before I could answer, he said,
'How did the chicken turn out?'

I was startled.

'How did you know I'd cooked a chicken?'

He chuckled, the laugh turning to a wheezing cough.

'I saw your father walking past with it. I guessed

who'd sold it to him too. It must have been the toughest bird in Jordan.'

'It was tough,' I admitted. 'I thought it was the way I cooked it. I've never done a chicken before. I didn't really know what to do.'

I looked away. I didn't like Abu Ali knowing about the chicken. It was the first time I'd cooked one and I'd made a mess of it. It had been really hard, pulling off its feathers and cutting it up with my blunt knife. I'd cooked it with an onion, some salt and a bit of cinnamon that Aunt Zainab had let me take from her kitchen.

It didn't seem too bad to me but Tariq had spat out bits of gristle and said, 'Why didn't you do it properly, like Auntie Shirin did? This doesn't taste of anything.'

Abu Ali was still watching me, his eyes bright with understanding. 'You're a good girl,' he said. 'And I tell you what, I've got some cakes left over from yesterday. They're nice, but too stale to sell. They'll only go to my wife's chickens. I'll box them up. A little treat for you and that unworldly Baba of yours?'

I was too embarrassed to answer right away. Tariq would have stiffened up and said, 'We don't need charity, thank you very much,' but Tariq wasn't there. He'd have been wrong, anyway, because we did need charity. I'd nearly used up the supplies Aunt Zainab had given me when we'd moved into the tent. I'd asked Baba for money several times, but he'd only been able to give me a little, and I knew he'd had to borrow it from Uncle Yasser.

Sometimes he brought a few things with him when he came back from town, but he didn't know about shopping properly and they were never what we needed.

I looked at the cakes and my mouth watered.

'Thank you very much, Abu Ali,' I said, but as he put them into a box and slid the box into a plastic bag, I kept looking over my shoulder, hoping that no one would come in and see.

I turned to the door, the bag swinging from my hand, but he called me back.

'You didn't come in for cakes, did you, Miss Head-in-the-clouds? What's bothering you? Lost your best diamond ring?'

He said it in such a funny way that I had to smile.

'She wants coffee,' I said.

'Oh, does she?'

I knew he didn't think much of Aunt Zainab. I'd been in the shop with her several times, and seen the way she treated him.

'And — and she said — she asked — please can you make sure the beans are fresh.'

He frowned, running a hand over his bald head, which was fringed above the ears with bubbly white curls.

'She didn't say it like that, I don't suppose. But since you've asked so nicely, yes, you're in luck today. Fresh beans, just in. And there's a special offer on them too. Would you believe it? A chocolate bar with every five hundred grams.'

And, before I could object, he'd picked up a brightly coloured stick of chocolate and tucked it into my bag.

I was feeling rebellious when I went back into the house.

If Aunt Zainab says anything mean, I told myself, *I'm just going to tell her what a nasty old bag she is.*

'Here's the coffee, Aunt,' I said, handing over the packet and holding out her change. I was glaring at her but of course she didn't notice.

She held the packet to her nose and sniffed it.

'Abu Ali said the beans were fresh in today,' I said, trying not to sound angry.

'Much better than last week,' she pronounced at last. 'I told you, Safiya, you have to insist.'

I held out her change. She shot a sideways look at Um Salim.

'Keep it. Buy a little treat for yourself.'

Um Salim nodded approvingly, but I wasn't going to be patronized. I could hear Lamia's voice on the other side of the house, singing something tuneless as she played with her doll. I put the money down on the table, not trusting myself to speak, and hurried back out of the door.

'You see?' Aunt Zainab's voice followed me as I crossed the courtyard. 'No gratitude.'

CHAPTER THIRTEEN

It was still only late morning. There were hours to fill before Tariq got home from school, and I had no idea where Baba was. I knew I should be sweeping out the tent or washing shirts or finding something to cook for supper, but I felt too miserable to do anything.

I haven't got a friend in the world, I told myself bitterly. *Where are you, Saba? I need you!*

A rustling sound by the open tent flap made me look round.

A little white cat was pawing at the plastic bag full of Abu Ali's cakes.

'Oh, you lovely little thing!' I said. 'Where did you spring from?'

Back home, I'd adored Tiger, our old cat. He'd always been there when I got back from school. He used to jump off the courtyard wall and weave his tail round my legs. I'd throw handfuls of dead leaves in the air, and laugh at him batting them with his front paws.

I lifted the bag of cakes out of the cat's reach and hung it on a tent pole with the rest of the food.

'Sorry,' I told her apologetically, 'but these aren't for you.'

I bent down and lifted her up. She was so thin that I could feel the bones through her fur. She mewed and wriggled in my hands then turned her head and licked my finger with her rasping tongue.

'I'm going to call you Snowball,' I said.

I set her down, poured some water into a bowl and put it outside the tent flap. She sniffed at it, then dipped her head and lapped thirstily.

I lifted down the bag of cakes and looked inside. The chocolate bar! Kind old Abu Ali! I had a sort of friend, after all.

I tore the wrapping off the bar. I hadn't had any chocolate for ages and I ate it all in one go while the cat sniffed around the tent, investigating the rumpled edge of canvas where it sagged over the ground. I smoothed a bit out to make a bed for her. She inspected it for a moment or two, then flopped down and began to purr.

Snowball had cheered me up. I was ready to start my chores and began collecting up the dirty shirts. I took them out to the water tank, filled a bucket and put them in with some of the detergent Aunt Zainab had given me when we'd moved into the tent. I stirred the clothes around, then left them to soak.

Sweeping out the tent was the next job, and the one I hated most. Masses of dirt crept into the tent every day and grit got caught in the woven matting, even though we always took off our shoes when we came in and left them by the open flap. It took forever to clean up.

When I'd finished at last, I looked at my watch. Tariq would be home soon. What could I make for supper? There was just enough for pasta for the three of us, though Tariq, who was always hungry, would grumble and ask for more. I had an onion I could chop up and some tomato puree to make a sauce. All the rice had gone, and we'd eaten up the lentils too. There was one tin of beans left, some tea and that was just about it. We'd have to have pasta tonight. Again.

I was stirring the pasta on the little stove outside the tent when Baba came in through the gate. He frowned when he saw me, and said, 'How long have you been here on your own, Safiya? You really must be more careful. The tent's not a safe place for you. When Tariq and I are out, you must go to the house.'

But if I'm at Aunt Zainab's all day long, I thought, *who's going to wash your clothes, sweep the floor and cook the supper?*

Aloud, I said, 'Yes, Baba. I was there earlier. I came back to make the supper.'

The sad look I hated settled on his face.

'You should be at school. You shouldn't have to do all this.'

'Someone has to,' I said, more sharply than I'd intended. 'And I'm studying as much as I can, from Tariq's books. The ones he leaves back here.'

It wasn't true, but I knew it would please him.

Anyway, I keep meaning to, I thought. *I'll start soon.*

I saw his smile and took my opportunity.

'Baba, there's almost no food left. We're having the last of the pasta tonight. I need to do the shopping for tomorrow.'

He didn't seem to have heard me.

'Please, Baba,' I insisted. 'There isn't even any bread for breakfast.'

He looked at me despairingly.

'I've used all the cash Yasser lent me, and I've been trying and trying to get the bank in Azraq to transfer my account from Syria. Until I can sort it out, our money's frozen.'

He began to pace up and down inside the tumbledown fence, working himself up into a nervous state.

'I spend hours every day in queues and pleading with officials. They all say the same thing. "Go to Zarka. Everything has to go through the offices in Zarka!" How can I go to Zarka?' His voice was rising. 'It's hours on the bus. I'd have to go overnight. How can I leave you two here, on your own? Anyway, I don't even have enough money for the bus fare, never mind your bags of rice.'

Not my *bags of rice,* I thought resentfully. *Do you want to eat, or not?*

Now he was hitting himself on the forehead with the palm of his hand.

'I'll have to go back to Yasser and ask him for another loan.'

'No, Baba!' Neither of us had heard Tariq come. 'No more charity! Please! We don't need it now. Look, I don't know what you'll think about this, but I've got myself a job. Uncle Yasser says he needs another boy to work at his bottling plant. He's taken me on.'

Back home, he'd never have dared talk to Baba in that defiant way, but Baba looked more shocked than angry.

'Tariq! What are you thinking of!' he said. 'Your education! It's your whole future!'

Tariq crossed his arms over his chest.

'School ends at two. I'll work as hard as I can while I'm in class. The bottling plant's not far from school. It'll only take me ten minutes to get there. I'll have to work late when demand's high and all over the weekend, but Uncle Yasser says he'll pay me two JD a day. Three if I turn out to be any use. He was nice about it, Baba. He said he'd worked all his life, and – and you'd be proud of me.'

He ran out of confidence and shot me an anxious look. We waited, saying nothing.

At last Baba said, 'I *am* proud of you, Tariq. But your education! If that suffers, what sort of future can you have? Carrying water bottles around for the rest of your life?'

'I told you, Baba. I'll study all I can. I'm already the best in my class.'

Baba said nothing and went into the tent. Tariq punched the air, looking revoltingly pleased with himself. I squatted down beside the primus stove to test if the pasta was ready.

'Lucky you, being able to get a job,' I said jealously. 'Earning money. You make me feel useless.'

He sat down beside me.

'Don't say that. You couldn't work in the bottling plant, anyway. You have to be really strong. Specially your arms.'

He clenched a fist and raised it to make his muscles bulge. In spite of myself, I couldn't help laughing.

'Move over, Superman. Tariq's taking over!'

Then I wished I hadn't mentioned Superman. It was painful to remember how we'd watched those movies at home, slumped on our comfy old sofa.

Neither of us said anything for a while, then I dragged myself back to the present.

'Why do you have to be so strong, anyway?' I asked him. 'What do you have to do?'

'Load Uncle Yasser's truck with water bottles, then drive round with him, lift them down and deliver them to customers in shops and houses. You have to go really fast, run upstairs with the bottles sometimes, one in each hand.'

I thought of the huge, heavy container of drinking water that I kept inside the tent, which Uncle Yasser supplied free of charge. It was too heavy for me to lift.

'You'll never be able to do it,' I said. 'You're not strong enough.'

He looked insulted.

'I am! And, anyway, Uncle Yasser says I'll get better at it with practice. He says he can't treat me any differently from the other two boys he's got working there. "You work, I'll pay," he said. "You don't work, I won't pay." Suits me. No more begging, Safiya. We've got to stand on our own feet.'

I said nothing, thinking guiltily of Abu Ali's cakes, which were still hanging from the tent pole in their blue plastic bag. Tariq bent over the tomato sauce, enjoying the smell.

'It's only pasta again,' I said. 'And tomato sauce. There's not enough, but it's all the food that's left. And there are some cakes. Abu Ali – sold them to me cheap because they're stale.' I didn't like lying, but I was sure he wouldn't notice. 'I didn't have any money for bread. I asked Baba, but he hadn't got any either. You'll have to have cake for breakfast. I'm sorry. I . . .'

He grinned at me.

'Cake for breakfast sounds OK. Anyway, I'll be paying for our food from now on. Uncle Yasser's so great. He's doing his best for us.'

'I know,' I said unhappily. 'It's only . . .'

'Her.'

'Yes, her. And little Princess Lamia.'

He stood up and stretched luxuriously.

'My last evening of freedom. Hurry up with supper. I'm starving.'

'And you still will be when you've eaten it,' I retorted, taking the pan off the stove.

I was spooning out the pasta when Baba smacked his hands down on his knees and said, 'That's it. I've made up my mind. I'm going to ask Yasser if he knows anyone who can give me a lift to Zarka. I'll leave tomorrow if I can, stay over one night, and push as hard as possible to get my documents in order. To make a start. I should have done it a long time ago.'

He had straightened up and now he smoothed his hair back with the palm of his hand and smiled at us. For a moment he looked like the old Baba and my heart lifted. But then I had a scary thought. Tariq and I would have to spend a night in the tent alone. Tariq might pretend to be tough, but he was only fifteen, and a bit weedy, to be honest. With Baba away, all we'd have to protect us would be a rickety fence and thin canvas walls. Baba wasn't exactly the Incredible Hulk either, but at least he was a grown-up, and he would have died to protect us.

Now he was talking again.

'You two,' he said, stabbing a finger at each of us in turn, 'are going to spend tomorrow night at your uncle's house.' He looked at his watch. 'Six o'clock. We'll eat first, then I'll go over and talk to Yasser.'

*

It was dark when we'd finished our supper. I went outside
to fetch the solar lamp, which had been charging all day
in the sun, and hung it up from the tent pole. Then I took
down the cakes and handed them round, holding some
back for breakfast.

Something had changed. There was a sort of energy in
both Baba and Tariq. They made me feel even more small
and powerless.

I wish I was a boy, I thought.

After Baba had gone over to the house, Tariq settled
down under the lamp with his books.

'Listen,' I said. 'I heard Aunt Zainab and Um Salim
talking about our mother today.'

He looked up sharply.

'Did you?'

'Do you remember her at all?'

'No. Well – just a sort of feeling of someone holding
me, I think. And a kind of smell. Sweet. Why? What did
they say?'

I made a face.

'Nothing much. Aunt Zainab said she hadn't liked
Mama, but I don't know if she likes anyone much.'

Neither of us spoke for a moment. Then I said, 'You
are lucky, Tariq.'

'Me? Why?'

'You had her for two years.'

'I know, but—'

I rushed on, cutting him off.

'The awful thing is that I suppose it was sort of my fault – mine and Saba's – that she died. I mean, because of our birth.'

He shook his head vigorously.

'That's daft, Safiya. It was nobody's fault. Auntie Shirin would have said it was the will of Allah. It happened. That's all.'

'So you . . .' I swallowed. 'You don't blame me?'

'No, silly! Of course I don't! I mean, you can be the most annoying person in the whole world, but . . .'

He had to duck to avoid the tea towel I flung at his head, and we both burst out laughing.

CHAPTER FOURTEEN

It was still dark when I woke up the next morning. Baba was up already. I could hear splashes outside as he washed behind the screen near the water tank.

He came back into the tent and started filling a pan from the drinking-water bottle.

I crawled out of bed.

'I'll make your tea, Baba. You get ready to go.'

I went outside and set the pan on to boil. The first streaks of daylight were already running in faint stripes through the open flap across the straw mats on the tent floor. By the time Tariq was up and dressed, I had the tea ready. Baba was dragging a comb through his hair.

'Where will you stay tonight, Baba?' I asked, giving him one of the last of the cakes.

'An old client from Damascus. He'll put me up.'

'And you'll get supper there?'

He pinched my cheek.

'Don't worry about your old Baba, *habibti*. I'll eat like a king tonight.'

I turned my head, not wanting him to see that I was hurt.

'Lucky you,' muttered Tariq. Then he caught my eye. 'What are you looking at me like that for?'

There was a crunch of wheels on the stony ground outside and a car horn beeped.

'Here's my lift,' said Baba, draining the last of his tea.

He went outside, then poked his head back through the tent flap.

'You're starting at the bottling plant today?' he asked Tariq.

'Yes.'

'Take it easy. You could strain your back if you go at it too hard at first.'

He was almost at the gate before he remembered me.

'Go to your aunt today, Safiya,' he called back.

Then he was gone.

I shuffled into my shoes and went outside to rinse Baba's tea glass. I got back to the tent in time to see Tariq pick up the last cake and ate it. Neither of them had thought to leave one for me. I was just about to explode when he said, 'Baba's right. You'll have to spend the day with her. Good luck. At least she'll give you lunch.'

I realized that he might not have anything else to eat all day and I stopped being angry.

Uncle Yasser's truck started up outside. Tariq grabbed his schoolbag and dived for the gate.

'Hope it goes well!' I called after him. 'When will you be . . .' but he didn't hear me above the roar of the truck's engine.

I retied the loop of wire that fastened the gate to the tent post, then turned back to the dreary tent, sagging on its ropes.

See what I mean, Saba? I asked my absent twin. *They don't care about me at all. Go ahead, Baba. Eat like a king tonight. See if I care.*

Unwillingly, I set about tidying the tent, folding the blankets and picking up dirty clothes to wash.

And then, taking me by surprise, I felt as if someone had touched my shoulder, and I heard a woman's voice say, 'You're looking after them for me, Safiya. You're the heart of the family now.'

'Mama!' I called out. 'I wish, I *wish* you were here! Why won't Baba talk about you? Why won't he tell me what you were really like?'

But the sense of her presence had gone almost as soon as it had come.

Snowball came worming through a gap in the fence. She trotted up to me and butted my leg with her head.

'Sorry, Snowball. There's nothing for breakfast. I'll get you some clean water, though.'

She strutted into the tent, lapped from the water bowl, then stretched out in her sleeping place and went to sleep.

She could have gone anywhere, I thought, *but she chose me.*

I bent down and tickled her under the chin, then forced myself to go behind the screen by the water tank for a good wash.

Not having a bathroom was the worst thing about living in the tent. I just couldn't get used to it. At home, our lovely bathroom had blue tiles with white fishes embossed on them, a hot shower, piles of soft towels and rows of gels and shampoos. Now all I had was a bucket of cold water, some cheap soap and a tin mug to use as a dipper. Now that summer was nearly over, it was starting to get chilly in the mornings and the cold water made me shiver.

My hair needed washing, but I couldn't face it.

I'll do it tomorrow, I promised myself.

I'd tidied up the tent and was putting on my hijab, ready to go over to the house, when there was a knock on the gate.

'Safiya, where are you?'

It was Aunt Zainab.

What do you want now? I thought nervously.

She'd never been in the tent before. Had she come to inspect it?

'Coming, Aunt,' I called back, running to the gate.

She trod carefully across the rough ground towards the tent as if she was afraid of stepping in something nasty then she kicked off her shoes and walked right in. Her eyes swept across the blankets I'd folded neatly on the mattresses and the clothes I'd hung up tidily from the tent poles. If she was looking for something to criticize, she was going to be disappointed.

'You need to keep your food off the floor,' she said at last, then stopped. 'Where *is* your food?'

'It's – it's all finished, Aunt. We had the last of the pasta yesterday.'

She frowned.

'Why don't you go to Abu Ali's?'

I flushed with shame.

'Baba – I – no money,' I mumbled.

'What? Speak up!'

'Baba didn't have any money to give me.'

I was sure I saw a spark of triumph in her eyes.

'Silly girl. Why didn't you come and ask me? Your uncle would never let you starve.'

I'm not going to beg if that's what you want, I thought angrily.

'Thank you, Aunt,' I said stiffly, 'but Tariq's working now. He's going to give me what he earns. I'll go to Abu Ali tomorrow.'

'What? You can't live on three JD a day!' She took another look around the tent. 'This isn't how you expected life to be, is it, Safiya? I suppose you had the best of everything in Syria. Lovely clothes, eating in nice restaurants, a smart car . . . Your family always liked expensive things.'

My face burned. How dared she talk about us like that? Surely she couldn't be jealous? Not after all that had happened to us?

'You had a maid, I suppose, in Damascus,' she went

on. 'I bet your aunt never had to do any housework. Did she even cook?'

I was finding it hard to keep my temper.

'Auntie Shirin's food is wonderful,' I said coldly.

'No need to get upset. I was only asking. I hope she taught you to cook, now that you're in charge here.'

'No, she didn't.' I just wanted the conversation to end. 'I'm managing.'

She frowned for a moment, then said, 'You know what, Safiya, life is full of disappointments. I was married when I was fifteen. If your father's got any sense, he'll soon get you married too. That's the end of any silly dreams you might have. You have to learn the hard way, like I did. Your life isn't how you expected it to be, and that's that.'

'I think I know that already, Aunt,' I said, flushing.

'Yes, well, perhaps you're learning it at last. You thought you were something when you came to Jordan, didn't you? You'd never swept a floor in your life. But you're the same as everyone else who has to make their way in the world.'

I felt winded. She'd knocked the breath right out of me. But the next thing she said took me by surprise.

'I suppose I could teach you a few things myself. I'm thought to be rather a good cook, actually.'

She waited. I knew what was expected.

'Your cooking is wonderful too, Aunt Zainab,' I said. 'That first night, when we arrived, I'll never forget the lovely things you made for us.'

She could see I meant it. She even smiled.

'You're doing your best, I suppose. You're managing better than I'd expected, as a matter of fact. Come on. We'll go to Abu Ali's first and do the shopping.'

She ducked her head to go out through the tent opening and caught sight of Snowball, lounging on her sleeping place.

'Shoo!' She flapped her arms and clapped her hands. 'Get out! Go on!'

'It's all right!' I said quickly. 'I don't mind her. She's very clean. And – and –' I was casting around for a clincher. 'She keeps the rats away.'

Aunt Zainab shuddered.

'Rats! Well . . .' She glanced back into the tent, looking for something to criticize. 'You've left your solar lamp inside. You have to put it in the sun to recharge.'

I scowled at her back.

I'm not a total idiot, I thought. *I hadn't got round to it when you barged in here.*

She hadn't finished.

'If there are rats around, you need a secure place to store your food. I've got an old tin trunk that I don't need any more. I'll fetch it out for you.'

I picked up the solar lamp, set it out in the sun, then started tying the flap of the tent shut, bending over so that she couldn't read the expression on my face.

'Thank you, Aunt. That's very good of you,' I said.

CHAPTER FIFTEEN

I didn't like going into Abu Ali's shop with Aunt Zainab.
She was so snobbish and rude. Abu Ali knew how I felt. He
waited till she was bent over the aubergines, inspecting
one after another, then he winked at me. By the time
she'd turned round his face was a blank.

'Don't just stand there,' Aunt Zainab said to me. 'Go
and pick out two cans of fava beans. And mind you check
the sell-by dates.'

Another woman came into the shop, and Aunt Zainab's
manner changed completely.

'Muna, my dear! How are you? How is everyone?
What's the news of that son of yours in America?'

They plunged into a noisy conversation. I put the two
cans of beans down on Abu Ali's counter. He leaned over
it and said in a quiet voice, 'Don't run away, miss. I want
to talk to you.'

'What about?'

'I know your situation,' he said. 'You're a brave girl.
Allah sees it all. He knows that everyone needs help from
time to time.'

He's going to offer me charity! I thought nervously,

imagining the expression on Tariq's face.

'Thank you, Abu Ali, but I . . .' I began.

He put up his hand to stop me talking.

'There's an organization that helps refugee families. They're good people. Why refuse? You can't help what's happened. A basic food box once a month. Cooking oil, pasta, rice, tea, cans of this and that. I can help you register with them.'

I nearly jumped with relief. Yesterday I'd been so thrilled at the thought of the money Tariq would be bringing in that I'd stopped worrying about how I was going to pay for our food. But just now, looking round Abu Ali's shop, I'd been doing the sums in my head. Aunt Zainab had been right. Three JD a day wouldn't go far at all.

'You – you mean all those things, every single month?'

'Yes. Every month.'

Then, as if he was standing beside me, I heard Tariq's voice in my head. *No charity!*

Over by the vegetables, Aunt Zainab and her friend were embracing.

'So you'll come on Saturday?' the other woman was saying. 'Bring that pretty daughter of yours.'

I'll deal with you later, I silently told Tariq.

Aloud, I said, 'Thank you Abu Ali. I can't tell you – It would be so –'

He nodded.

'Good. Tell your Baba to come and see me. I'll get it sorted out.'

Aunt Zainab was bearing down on us, bags of vegetables in her hands.

'Tomato paste. Hurry up,' she said to me, waving her hand towards the back of the shop.

I went off to find it. The prices didn't look so scary now. With a food box of basics every month, and Tariq's money as well, I'd be able to do much better.

She says she'll teach me to cook, I thought. *All right, Aunt Zainab. I'll hold you to that. I'll be your obedient servant just till I've learned what I need to know. You can whistle for me as much as you like after that.*

Back at the house, I put the heavy bags down on the kitchen table while Aunt Zainab took off her hijab and poured herself a glass of water.

'I'll get started on tonight's supper,' she said. 'You can shake out all the rugs. Hang them up on the line in the courtyard and give them a good beating.'

I took a deep breath.

'You – you said you'd teach me to cook, Aunt Zainab.'

She frowned.

'Yes, but I didn't mean . . .'

'You're such a marvellous cook,' I gushed. 'I really want to learn from you.'

'Oh, all right,' she said at last. 'You can do the rugs later. We're having lentil and chard soup tonight.'

'I love that,' I said. 'Especially the way you make it.'

Careful, I told myself. *Don't overdo it.*

She was tossing back her thick, glossy hair.

'Well, get on with it, Safiya. Unpack the shopping first.' She watched as I darted around the kitchen, putting everything away. 'Now get out the large saucepan. Start by chopping the onions, and no complaints, please, if they make you cry.'

Aunt Zainab wasn't a bad teacher, actually. She didn't hover over me, but just gave me instructions and let me get on with it while she sat at the table flicking through the pages of a film magazine. Every now and then she'd look up and say things like, 'You're burning the onions. Turn the heat down.' Or, 'You haven't washed those lentils properly. Do them again.'

It was late when Uncle Yasser and Tariq came home. Tariq looked so tired that his face had gone grey. He flopped down on the cushions as I brought out the soup and bread and laid them on the cloth on the floor. Aunt Zainab served them out. I waited for her to say, 'Safiya cooked the supper tonight,' but of course she didn't.

No one said anything about the soup, but Tariq came back for three helpings, and Uncle Yasser took two.

As I was clearing the dishes away, Tariq put two fingers into the breast pocket of his shirt and pulled out three crumpled notes.

'Here you are,' he said, grinning. 'Three JD.'

I tucked them away in my own pocket and at that moment I think I felt as proud of him as he felt of himself.

CHAPTER SIXTEEN

Tariq and I slept on the cushions in the sitting room that night. Even though I was really tired, I lay awake for a long time. Something was bothering me, something I'd heard Um Salim say to Aunt Zainab. *Awful what happened, wasn't it?* she'd said. And Aunt Zainab had replied, *You could have seen it coming. I always thought she was a bit . . . you know . . .*

What could Aunt Zainab have seen coming? What had she meant? What was it that no one had told me?

'Tariq,' I whispered. 'Are you awake? I really want to ask you something.'

A light snore was my only answer.

When at last I did go to asleep, I fell into a dream.

For the first time in my life, I dreamed about my mother. She was wearing her wedding dress, like in the picture in Baba's bedroom. She looked stiff and pale, as if she was made of wax.

'I had to go away,' she said, in a voice that was surprisingly strong.

'Is it really you, Mama? Why did you leave me? You're dead, aren't you?' I cried out.

She smiled sadly at me.

'Go on,' she said.

'What do you mean, go on? Go on doing what?'

'Just go on.'

She walked away. I tried to follow her, but something was tangled round my feet. She turned a corner and disappeared.

Someone was shaking me.

'What's the matter with you?' Tariq was saying. 'You were crying in your sleep.'

'Nothing. A dream,' I mumbled.

He flopped back on to the cushions and was asleep again at once.

CHAPTER SEVENTEEN

The next afternoon I was in Aunt Zainab's courtyard and had just finished hanging out her washing when I heard the clang of our gate.

'Baba's home!' I called out to her, and dashed off to the tent.

Baba looked tired.

'How did it go? Did you get our money?' I asked him.

He shook his head.

'It'll take a long time. At least I've made a start.'

He sat down on his mattress.

'Sit here with me. I've got something to tell you.'

What now? I thought. *No more shocks, please, Baba!*

'Listen, *habibti*,' he said. 'You remember my half-brother Malik? He came to stay with us a few times in Damascus.'

'Uncle Malik?' I said, puzzled. 'Of course I do. What made you think of him?'

Malik was the odd one out in Baba's family. His father, my grandfather, had married a second wife when he'd been quite old. She'd been very young and from a poor family. No one in Baba's family had approved.

'So common,' Auntie Shirin used to say. 'So uneducated. What was our father thinking?'

She'd been scornful of Malik too. Looking back, I could understand why Malik had been so shy when he'd come to visit us. He was only a few years older than Tariq and we'd been horrible to him, teasing him all the time. Auntie Shirin had never stopped us, but even though she despised Malik she still made us call him 'Uncle' when we spoke to him. She was always like that. We had to be proper and show respect, even when we didn't feel it.

'Would you believe it — Malik's here in Jordan. In Zarka!' Baba went on. 'I bumped into him yesterday, walking down the street. The most extraordinary coincidence! He looked a bit lost, actually. He had to get out of Syria in a hurry, like we did. He's coming to live with us here.'

I stared at Baba, stunned.

'But we haven't even got enough food for ourselves!' I burst out. 'And where's he going to sleep?'

He put a hand on my knee.

'He's our family, Safiya. My own brother. I feel bad about the way we treated him and his mother. She was just a child, you know. Years younger than us. Your aunt resented her. But we've got to forget all that now. Malik won't make things more difficult for us. He's been working as a builder or an electrician or something. He'll get work in Azraq and pay his way. And we'll screen off part of the tent just for you, so you can have a sort of private room. Malik will sleep in the main area, with Tariq and me.'

It was all decided. There was nothing I could do.

'When's he coming, Baba?' I said in a small voice.

'He'll be here by supper time.'

He put his hand in his pocket and pulled out some money.

'My old client, the one I stayed with last night, reminded me that he hadn't paid me for my last consultation with him. Here, go off and buy what you need for supper.'

'All right, Baba,' I said. 'But I need you to come with me. Abu Ali wants to ask you something, and I really need you to say yes.'

Abu Ali was chasing a couple of skinny little boys out of his shop.

'*Yalla!* Shoo! Go off to your mothers!' he was shouting, pretending to scowl furiously. 'No more sweets for you today!'

They pushed past us in the doorway and ran off, laughing.

'*Ahlan wa sahlan, ya Abu Tariq,*' Abu Ali said politely. 'You are welcome.'

Baba's eyebrows rose.

'You know my name?'

Abu Ali laughed.

'Of course! Everyone knows everything around here. You are Tariq's father. And this is your daughter too.' He leaned forward over the counter. 'Actually, sir, I'm glad of the chance to speak to you.'

'What about?' said Baba. He saw that I was listening. 'Go and do your shopping, Safiya.'

I went off unwillingly to look along the dusty shelves for what I needed. Their quiet voices faded as I collected the ingredients I'd need to make the soup Aunt Zainab had taught me.

I've just got to show them all that I can cook something nice, I told Saba in my head. *You'd feel the same. I know you would.*

I went back to the counter feeling pleased with myself, but my heart sank when I saw the expression on Baba's face.

'Did you ask Abu Ali for help, Safiya, without my permission?'

I felt my face flush angrily.

'No, Baba! Of course I didn't! How could you think—'

'She didn't need to,' Abu Ali interrupted. 'Look, sir, there's no shame in taking what's freely given. All gifts come from Allah. I'm sure you yourself, when times were better, gave money to charity.'

Baba grunted.

'Of course, but . . .'

'There's a time to give, and a time to receive,' Abu Ali went on. '*Inshallah*, when all these troubles are over, you will give back ten times more than the small amount you are offered now.'

Baba was hesitating, I could tell. I grabbed his sleeve.

'Baba, please. I can't ask Aunt Zainab for anything more. She makes it so hard. Just to have the basic things every month! And then, with Tariq's money, I can manage all right. There's nothing left in the tent, Baba. I gave you the last of the tea just now.'

Baba said nothing for a moment, then he patted my arm and turned back to Abu Ali.

'We'll accept with – with gratitude,' he said stiffly, as if the words were burning his mouth. 'Your kindness is . . .'

Then I felt embarrassed because he had to turn away to hide his tears.

CHAPTER EIGHTEEN

As soon as we got back from Abu Ali's, Baba pulled out a roll of old canvas that had come with the tent and which had been lying behind the mattresses.

'I thought we could use this to make a screen for you,' he said, looking at it doubtfully. 'We'll hang it up between the tent poles.'

I wrinkled my nose.

'What's that awful smell?'

He felt the canvas with his hand.

'It's a bit musty, that's all. Must have got damp.'

'It stinks, Baba.'

'It'll air off. Come on, Safiya. Lift up that end. And you'll need to fetch in your washing line from outside. We'll have to sling it over that.'

'But, Baba, how am I going to hang out the washing?' I asked him, trying to keep the edge out of my voice.

He looked exasperated.

'One thing at a time. Just go and fetch the rope.'

I was shaking my head as I went outside. Baba might have been the most brilliant lawyer ever, but no one could have called him a handyman.

I was working at the tight knot that held the washing line to the stand of the water tank when I heard someone knocking on the gate. I went to open it.

If I hadn't been expecting Malik, I don't think I'd have recognized him. The boy I'd known years ago had been chubby and pale, so flabby that he could hardly run.

'Dreadfully spoiled,' Auntie Shirin used to say. 'That woman treats him like a little prince. Lets him play computer games and watch TV all day long.'

Malik was still short, of course, and his round head still sat straight down on his shoulders as if he had no neck at all, but now he was terribly thin. The skin down one side of his face was puckered and red. His hands, once so soft and plump, looked hard and rough. His adoring mama had always bought him the best of everything, new clothes and shoes all the time. Now he wore a workman's stained, worn jeans, splashed with white paint, the cuffs of his jacket were frayed and I could smell the old sweat on his shirt from metres away.

He was staring at me as hard as I was staring at him.

I suppose I've changed a lot too, I thought uncomfortably.

'Safiya?' he said at last.

Aloud I said, as warmly as I could, 'Uncle Malik, is that you? *Ahlan wa sahlan.* You are welcome.'

Baba hurried out of the tent, ducking under the low entrance, and nearly tripping over the loose canvas that was crumpled all over the tent floor.

'This is wonderful, Malik!' he exclaimed. 'However

did you find us so quickly?'

'You gave me directions,' said Malik simply, running his tongue over his dry lips as if he was unsure of his welcome.

'Come in, come in,' said Baba, taking the battered backpack off Malik's shoulders. 'We're living very plainly, as you see. But you're welcome, of course. We all have to – things are very – Safiya, help me roll up this canvas. We'll fix it up later. Sit down, Malik, please. What's the latest news from Syria? It's so hard to find out anything here.'

I left them to it and went outside to make my soup. It took longer than I'd expected to get everything done. Once it was merrily boiling on the little stove I went back inside and was surprised to see that the screen was up. The tent looked quite different.

'You didn't use my washing line, after all,' I said, peering up in the dim light to see how it had been done.

'We didn't need to,' Baba said enthusiastically. 'I hadn't noticed those little holes running along the edge of the canvas. And those loops hanging down? Malik worked it all out. Look! Now you've got your own little room.'

I tried to look grateful, but I wasn't at all. I'd just started to feel that I could cope with everything, but now that Malik had come I felt invaded.

I suppose Aunt Zainab feels about us the way I feel about Malik, I thought uncomfortably.

You'd never swept a floor in your life till you came to Jordan, had you? she'd said. She must have thought that I was as spoiled as Malik had been.

Baba was smiling at me expectantly.

'It's wonderful, thank you,' I said in a colourless voice, and I gathered up my few possessions, which I'd been keeping in a corner of the tent, and took them into my canvas cubbyhole.

The soup was ready by the time I'd sorted everything out. I dished it out, dying to know if Baba and Malik would like it. I needn't have worried. Baba dug his spoon in deep, and Malik ate like someone who'd never seen food before. When he'd finished, he said, 'That was the best thing I've ever eaten in my life.'

I hid a triumphant smile as I refilled his bowl. Perhaps Malik wasn't such a bad thing, after all.

'When was your last meal, Malik?' asked Baba.

'Yesterday – no, the day before.'

My eyes opened wide with horror.

'Then it's just as well we met,' Baba said. 'You're with your family now.'

Malik looked as if he didn't believe him.

'You're very kind, Adnan,' he said formally.

Tariq came home as I was outside the tent rinsing the bowls.

'Wait,' I said, blocking his way. 'Listen. Uncle Malik's here.'

He tried to push me aside.

'What are you talking about? He can't be!'

'He is! Our very own baby-face uncle. Baba met him in Zarka. He's come to live with us.'

Even in the dark I could read the shock on Tariq's face.

'What? That fat lump? What's he doing here?'

'He's not fat any more. He's really skinny. He hadn't eaten anything for a couple of days. He's moved in with us. He's staying.'

'What?' said Tariq furiously. 'You mean he's going to scrounge off us? Safiya, he can't! I'm killing myself earning a pathetic three JD a day. It's not even enough for us!'

'Shh! He'll hear you.'

Tariq groaned.

'It's not exactly thrilling for me either,' I said tartly, 'but he's Baba's brother, after all.'

There was no answer to that.

'What's for supper?' he said, kicking his shoes off at the tent entrance.

'Lentil soup. Like yesterday.'

Even in the dark I could see his angry glare.

'Don't ask Aunt Zainab to give us food! You know I hate taking their stuff.'

'I didn't. I made it myself.' I couldn't keep the pride out of my voice. 'And *I* made last night's soup, which Aunt Zainab naturally failed to mention.'

'Yeah. Well.' He obviously didn't believe me. 'I hope there's plenty left, anyway. I'm starving.'

CHAPTER NINETEEN

The next day was Friday. At home, we'd always slept in on Friday mornings, and then I'd go round to spend the day with Farah. We'd listen to her music, try on her mama's make-up, giggle over nothing . . .

Stop remembering! I told myself. *Stop!*

I'd never been able to sleep late in the tent. Baba getting up had always woken me, and, anyway, my bed wasn't exactly the kind you'd snuggle into for a luxurious lie-in.

I'd thought I wouldn't sleep a wink in my canvas cubicle, but actually it had been all right once I'd got used to the smell. I had to admit it was nice having my own space, even though it was tiny. It was less draughty too.

As soon as breakfast was over, Tariq sighed and got out his schoolbooks.

'Aren't you going to the bottling plant today?' I asked him.

'Yes, but not till eleven. I've got a mass of homework to catch up with this morning.'

Baba was by the entrance, putting on his shoes.

'Well, Malik, are you ready?' he said. 'I'll take you across to meet Yasser.'

'It's just – I only have these clothes,' Malik said, looking nervous. He had scrambled awkwardly to his feet and was looking down at his stained, splashed jeans and dirty shirt.

'Oh, that doesn't matter,' Baba said breezily. 'They're family.'

But it does matter, I thought, frowning. *Aunt Zainab will notice everything.*

I was still clearing away the breakfast things when I heard a car draw up outside. The door banged, then someone knocked on the gate. Tariq, who was scowling over his maths book, didn't look up, so I went to open it myself.

A man stood there with a carton in his hand.

'Mr Adnan?' he said.

I pointed with my chin to Uncle Yasser's house.

'My father's over there.'

He held the carton out to me.

'Can I leave it with you? I've got loads more deliveries to make.'

'What is it?'

He looked surprised.

'Weren't you expecting it? It's your monthly food box. From the refugee charity.'

Behind me I heard a sharp, *'What?'* from Tariq.

'*Alf shukr.* Thank you very much,' I said quickly, willing

him to go away before Tariq could intervene.

To my relief he turned and ran back to his car, jumped in and drove off. In the rear window, I could see more boxes piled up high. I shut the gate just as Tariq stormed up to me.

'Who was that? Did he say charity? A refugee *charity*? What on earth have you been doing?'

He was trying to snatch the carton out of my hands. I held it tightly to my chest. Fury boiled up inside me.

'Get off!' I snarled. 'Don't you dare touch it!'

He looked as if he was actually going to fight me for it.

'I've told you, Safiya, again and again! No charity! How dare you sneak off behind my back and—'

'And you can just shut up!' I yelled back at him. 'Baba knows about this. He agreed. I didn't ask for anything!'

'Oh no?' He was sneering now. 'All that food you took off Aunt Zainab last night—'

'How *dare* you!' I was scarlet with rage. 'I bought the vegetables from Abu Ali and cooked them myself. I used your money and a bit that Baba was paid in Zarka from a client he met there. It was Abu Ali who told Baba about the monthly box thing. You ask him. Or is it you who's running everything around here now?'

He backed away.

'All right. No need to go crazy. I'll talk to Baba. If all this was his mad idea . . .'

The box was so heavy that my arms were aching. I put it down on the ground.

'Right. You do that. Then you tell me how I'm supposed to manage on three JD a day.'

He shrugged.

'We've managed up to now. We—'

'Yes, on the food Aunt Zainab gave us as a start-up. And it's not just food we need. I suppose you want your clothes washed? We've run out of detergent. Soap? There's almost none left. Toothpaste? Clean your teeth with sand if you like. There's loads of it around here. What about a new gas bottle for the stove? You want me to dream it out of thin air? And Baba's socks. Have you noticed them? More hole than sock. This box is a life-saver. I'm not exaggerating. You tell me, Tariq. How are we to manage without it? Go on. Tell me.'

He was backing away still further.

'All right. Calm down. There's no need to—'

'There is, actually. You've got to understand. There's something Abu Ali said. He asked Baba if he used to give money away to charity. Of course Baba did. A lot. You know that. "There's a time to give," Abu Ali said, "and a time to receive." So get this, Tariq. Now is the time to receive.'

'Wow!' Tariq put his hands up in surrender. 'All right, little sister. I give in. But . . .'

'But what?'

He actually grinned at me.

'But nothing. I don't dare say another word. By the way, did you really make that soup?'

'Yes, I did. And if you don't believe me—'

'I do! I do! All I wanted to say was that it was good. Really good. Can I go back to work now, please?'

I should have said, *Do what you like. It was you who started this row in the first place.* But I knew I'd won, so I just turned my back on him, and bent over to open the box.

CHAPTER TWENTY

There were voices outside and the gate opened.

'Careful, Malik,' Baba was saying. 'Don't bash your leg on this thing. The corners are really sharp.'

They came in carrying an old tin chest between them. It had been patterned all over in red and blue once, but the paint had mostly rubbed off and now it was covered in dents.

'Zainab says this is for you,' Baba said. Then he saw the tins and packets I'd taken out of the box. 'What's all this?'

'The – the refugee people,' I said, looking sideways at Tariq, who was watching through narrowed eyes. 'A man brought it after you'd gone.'

Baba nodded.

'Yes, well, all right.'

I shot Tariq a triumphant look as he and Malik settled down on a mattress to talk.

'Do you really think your cousin will help me find work?' began Malik anxiously.

'I'm sure he will.' Baba's voice was warm and kind. He almost sounded like his old self. 'But what I don't understand is how you came to be working on building sites for so long. Two years, you told Yasser! You're only eighteen. Surely you were still at school?'

There was an odd expression on Malik's face as he looked back at Baba, and he didn't answer.

'I'm sorry about the way we lost touch after our father died,' Baba went on, filling the awkward silence. 'It was a strange time for all of us.' He was starting to look embarrassed. 'Your mother went off with you so suddenly, before we had time to get used to the situation and decide what to do. I hope you didn't feel we'd abandoned you. It must have been – I suppose it was hard for your mother?'

'It was,' said Malik shortly.

There was another difficult silence. At last Malik said, 'My mother was miserable in Damascus with my father. Shirin, well, the whole family – they didn't like her.' Baba flinched, but Malik didn't notice. 'She was desperate to get back to her village and be with her own people.'

Baba leaned forward.

'At least – I'm sure – that our father left her well provided for, with money for your education?'

Malik looked down at his work-calloused hands.

'Mama's family were very poor. They'd more or less sold her to him in the first place. She was only fourteen. Years younger than you and Shirin. He was nearly fifty years older than her.'

I gasped. How awful it must have been for her, my poor little stepgrandmother, married off to an old man!

She'd been only two years older than me now! I didn't remember my stern grandfather very well. Tariq and I had kept out of his way when he and his second family came to see us, and Auntie Shirin had despised her stepmother so much that we had almost never visited them. Tariq and I had been horrible to Malik. How could we have been so cruel?

'Mama wasn't clever with money,' Malik went on in a low voice. 'Her brothers soon took it all off her, and left her with almost nothing.'

Baba was looking appalled.

'I had no idea! What did you do?'

Malik was hunched over his knees, not looking at any of us.

'There was nothing for us in the village. We went to the south. I got work on a building site. I'd never done anything like that before. Didn't have the muscles for it. It was — it got easier. I had a good boss. He taught me a lot. We managed.' He flexed his shoulders. 'I earned enough, just, to keep us.'

'But my dear Malik!' Baba sounded horrified. 'Why didn't you come to me? To us?'

Malik shot him a quick glance, then looked away.

'Mama didn't want . . . She thought that . . .'

There was an awkward silence.

'Of course we would have helped you! We would never have—'

'We didn't need your help, anyway,' Malik interrupted

stiffly. 'I was working. I looked after my mother myself.'

'But your education!'

'Oh that!' Malik shook his head. 'You know I'm not clever, like you lot are. I can't even read properly. The letters dance about on the page whenever I try. It's called dyslexia or something, but the teachers just said I was stupid and lazy. They punished me all the time.'

I caught Tariq's eye. He'd stopped pretending to do his homework and was biting his lip in shame.

'Actually,' Malik went on, 'I *liked* working on the building site once I'd got to be strong enough. I'm good at practical things. I learned brick-laying, carpentry, electrical work. For the first time in my life I knew what it was to work. It gave me — I don't know — self-respect.'

'And then?' prompted Baba.

'I was called up for military service. It was just about bearable at first. I'd learned by then to stand on my own feet. But when the trouble started . . .' He stopped.

'They put a gun in your hand and told you to shoot at other Syrians, at your own people,' Baba said harshly. 'It happened to every man in the army, and they all had to make the same decision. To shoot, or not to shoot.'

'What did you do?' asked Tariq.

'I couldn't shoot at people. I ran away.'

'Good for you,' said Tariq, shutting his book with a snap.

Malik shook his head.

'I was careless. I didn't plan it properly. They came

after me, of course. Caught me.' He shut his eyes. 'It was . . . I don't want . . .'

'But you got away again, didn't you?' I dared to ask.

'One of the guards, in the prison, he was a good guy. He helped me get out. I could only just walk after all the beatings. They burned my face too.' He touched the puckered skin on his cheek. 'There were others making for the border. I joined them. Got across into Jordan three weeks ago. People have helped me here and there. Not much to eat but –' he smiled shakily – 'my bruises are going down. Look.' He pulled up his sleeve to show us his arm. I could hardly bear to look at the huge yellow and purple blotches from his wrist right up to his elbow. He pulled his sleeve down again. 'If I hadn't met you yesterday, Adnan, I don't know what would have happened to me.'

He coughed to cover up the crack in his voice.

I was dying to know about his mother.

'Where's my – my grandmother?' I asked. 'Why didn't she come with you?'

'I didn't dare go to her,' Malik said. 'They'd have been watching for me. They'd have arrested her too.'

'But how's she managing? Who's looking after her?'

'I found her a job before I went into the army.' He looked round at us defiantly. 'She works in a school. She's a cleaner.'

'Oh, the poor thing!' I said unthinkingly.

'No,' Malik corrected me. 'The lucky thing. It's a good

job. My mother's not like you. She never went to school, she can't read and write, but she knows how to work. I'm proud of her, actually. I – I miss her very much.'

My heart lurched in sympathy.

'You'll find her again,' I blurted out. 'You'll be together again. When all this is over, and we go home, you'll . . .'

'I can never go back to Syria,' he interrupted. 'They'll never pardon a deserter from the army.'

'I'm glad Baba found you and brought you to us,' I said. 'It's funny to think you're our uncle and we never really knew you.'

He laughed.

'I don't feel very like your uncle. More like . . .'

'A brother maybe,' said Tariq gruffly. 'I'm glad you're here too.'

Malik looked from Tariq to me and back again as if to check that we meant what we said. Then he smiled shyly.

'I'm not going to be a burden to you. I'll make myself useful, I promise. I'm going to find work. There's lots of building going on around here. Your cousin – Yasser – what should I call him?'

'He's got a son called Fares, so call him Abu Fares,' said Baba.

'Yes, well, he said he'd help me.'

'He will too.' Tariq nodded. 'He's fair like that. If he says he'll do something, he does it.'

I moved my legs and hit the side of the tin trunk. It made a loud clang. Baba looked round.

'Why are you still here, Safiya? Why haven't you gone to thank your aunt?'

I scrambled to my feet.

'Sorry, Baba. I'll go now.'

I could smell onions frying as I went into Aunt Zainab's courtyard. She was cooking and the kitchen window was open.

'How many more of them are there going to be?' I heard her say. 'Are we going to have a refugee camp on our doorstep? You'll have to put your foot down, Yasser. Honestly . . .'

Uncle Yasser said something I couldn't hear.

'You're too soft!' I could just imagine how she was tossing her head. 'You saw him! Nothing but a common labourer! Adnan's own brother! So much for Mr High and Mighty now.'

She'd gone too far.

'That's enough, Zainab,' Uncle Yasser said sharply. 'The guy's been tortured. He's a good lad, I can tell.' He was on his high horse. 'You know what we've been taught. "A Muslim is not a Muslim who goes to bed satisfied while his neighbour is hungry." It's no more than our human duty to help them.'

Saucepans clattered as Aunt Zainab banged them down in her sink by way of an answer. The kitchen door into the courtyard opened and Uncle Yasser came out. He saw me and stopped, embarrassed.

He knows I heard her, I thought.

He fumbled in his pocket and brought out a banknote.

'I'm glad I've seen you, Safiya. You're always welcome at our house, you and your family. I hope you know that.'

He winced as another bang came from the kitchen. He pressed the banknote into my hand.

'Abu Ali's had a delivery of gas bottles today. Yours must be running out soon. Get yourself another one.'

I tried to give it back to him.

'Thank you, Uncle Yasser, but . . .'

'Don't be silly, *habibti*. Get your gas.' He raised his voice. 'Your father's a great man. He'll be himself again soon. And Tariq's a hard worker. You are too. I'm proud that you came to us.'

I was cross with myself after he'd gone. I'd been waiting all this time to catch him alone and ask him if he really had seen Uncle Hassan in Amman. I'd had my chance, and I'd missed it.

I'm sorry, Saba, I thought. *I haven't forgotten you, I promise.*

CHAPTER TWENTY-ONE

It had still been summer when we'd moved into the tent and the weather had been hot and dry, but autumn was coming now and storms were on their way.

A few days after Malik had arrived, huge dark clouds rolled across the sky, and thunder rumbled in the distance.

It was the middle of the morning. Baba was away in Zarka, Tariq was at school and Malik was sewing a button on to his jacket.

'Did your mother teach you to sew?' I asked him.

He smiled.

'No. She did everything like that for me. You know what mothers are.'

'I don't, actually.'

He looked up and saw my face.

'Sorry, Safiya.' There was an awkward silence. Then he said, 'You learn all that kind of stuff in the army.'

There was a ping as the first drop of rain hit the tent. More splattered down, then they all ran together as the rain fell like a waterfall.

Malik leaped to his feet and scanned the roof of the tent, looking for leaks. I darted outside to bring in my little cooking stove, then rushed back inside and was dropping the flap behind me to stop the rain driving in, when Malik pushed past me and went outside.

'What are you doing? You'll get soaked!' I shouted, above the drumming of the rain but he didn't answer. I peered out, gasping as the cold water hit my face. The sandy soil was saturated already and huge puddles were spreading fast.

I couldn't see Malik, but he suddenly came round from behind the tent carrying a short length of metal pole, which had been thrown away when the tent had been put up. He ran to the entrance and began digging.

'Are you crazy? Come inside!' I yelled at him.

He shouted back, 'We've got to dig a trench! The tent's going to flood! Pull the mattresses and everything else into the middle!'

He didn't have to tell me twice. I was already imagining how miserable it would be if our beds got wet. A few minutes later our mattresses, clothes and everything else we owned were in a jumble in the middle of the tent. I even dragged the tin food box over to join the rest, in case it had a hole in the bottom.

'I'll go round the edges and tell you where it's coming in!' I yelled at him.

I began to crawl round the walls of the tent, picking up the edges of the mat and tucking them away from the canvas. In the far corner, a puddle was already forming.

'Over here. This side,' I called out to Malik.

I could hear him splashing around outside.

'Can't see it,' he shouted. 'Bang the tent wall to show me!'

I pushed my fist against the canvas.

'Here! Look!'

A moment later I heard the scrape of the pole on the ground and Malik's grunts as he dug furiously at the hard earth. I watched for a moment as the water pooled away, but it was coming in already in several other places.

The storm can't have lasted for more than twenty minutes, but it seemed to go on forever. There were several more leaks, but Malik's frantic digging kept the worst of the water out. The rain stopped almost as soon as it had begun.

I expected Malik to come inside and change out of his wet clothes, and I'd already found some of Baba's for him to wear, but he stayed outside. I could hear him panting with effort as he went on digging.

I hitched the entrance flap open and a thin flash of white streaked through my legs. It was Snowball, looking half drowned, her wet fur clinging to her skinny body.

She miaowed pleadingly.

Quickly, I took some of yesterday's stale bread out of the food trunk, mixed a little milk powder with some water, and soaked the bread in it. She'd pushed her way past my hands before I'd finished. I couldn't stay and watch her eat. I wanted to see what Malik had done.

There was no point in putting shoes on. They'd have

been soaked in no time. I rolled my trouser legs up over my ankles and stepped outside, shuddering as cold water oozed between my toes.

The tent lay in what looked like a pool of glistening mud with puddles stretching to our makeshift fence. Malik splashed round from the far side of the tent, splattered with mud from head to foot.

'This thing's useless,' he said, throwing the metal pole aside. 'I need a spade. We've got to dig a deeper trench, a proper one, to keep the rain out. There'll be more storms now this weather's started.'

He was right. The trench was much too shallow. We needed to build up a little bank against the tent wall too.

'If you go round the tent again and loosen the earth with the pole, I'll scoop it out,' I said. 'It'll be softer now it's wet.'

He didn't answer, but wiped his mucky sleeve across his forehead, picked up the pole and got started.

I grabbed one of the pans Aunt Zainab had given me. It was useless for cooking because the handle was broken. I'd nearly thrown it out but I was glad now that I'd kept it. It would do for scooping mud.

We worked for what felt like hours. My back was soon aching, and my hands were chafed and raw, while my bare feet were numb with cold.

Malik straightened up at last.

'It might hold,' he said. 'Until the next downpour, at least.'

I flexed my sore back. The trench was still too shallow and the little bank wasn't high enough, but I was too wet and cold and tired to go on. The tent looked awful, sagging and splashed with mud, the earth all round it cratered with puddles.

'I hate it here!' I burst out. 'I just want to go home!'

'You look funny,' Malik said, trying to cheer me up although his teeth were chattering. 'Like you've been wallowing in a mud bath.'

It didn't cheer me up at all.

'And you look like you've crawled out of a pond,' I snapped back.

'Come on,' he said. 'Let's wash the mud off and get into dry clothes. And why don't I put the kettle on? We need a hot drink.'

CHAPTER TWENTY-TWO

I came out of my little room in dry clothes to find that Malik had put on Baba's old things. He looked more impressive, somehow.

'You know what,' I burst out. 'I'm really glad you're here! I'd have gone crazy if I'd been on my own. Everything would have got soaked.'

He didn't say anything, but made me sit down and poured out the tea.

When you're cold, a hot drink works like magic. I cupped the little glass in my hands, enjoying its warmth, and slowly my mood warmed up too.

What was it Mama had said when she'd come to me in my dream?

Go on, she'd said. *Go on*.

Did she prompt me to say what I said next? To find out the truth about her at last?

'You were five when I was born, weren't you?' I asked Malik.

He was pouring out more tea.

'Must have been. Five or six.'

'Do you remember my mother?'

He blew the steam away from the glass.

'I think so. She was nice. I liked her better than my own sister. Shirin was years older than me, and she never liked me, anyway.'

I steered him back to the subject.

'Nobody's ever said much about Mama. What was she like?'

He sipped his tea.

'I don't remember much. But it was sad what happened. With her illness and everything.'

'What illness? What are you talking about?'

'I thought you knew.'

'I don't know anything! Tell me!'

'They wanted to protect you, I suppose.' He'd started looking anxious. 'I don't know if I ought to say any more.'

'Protect me from what?'

'Well, it was so tragic. Don't get upset. I only know what my mother told me.'

'Yes, but what happened?'

He still hesitated. An insane hope almost took my breath away.

'She didn't die, did she? She's still alive somewhere. She . . .' He shook his head.

'No, no. She passed away. Honestly, I wish I'd never started all this. All I know is that she had a sort of breakdown. It happens sometimes to women after they've had a baby. Maybe it's harder with twins, I don't know.'

'Like she was crazy or something?'

My only picture of Mama was of the beautiful, laughing woman in Baba's wedding photo. It was as if the glass was cracking and the image was being distorted.

'Not crazy, Safiya,' Malik said gently. 'She had an illness. A mental illness.'

'All right. An illness. Go on! What happened!'

'I don't know much, only that she took Saba to Amman and died there.'

I felt like I'd been kicked in the stomach.

'She can't have done. She'd have taken me too. Anyway, Saba didn't go to Amman. My uncle took her to America. She had to have an operation.'

'I don't know about that. I'm only telling you what my mother said, and she probably got it wrong.'

'So how did she – Mama – how did she die?'

'I've no idea. Honestly, Safiya, I've told you everything I know.'

I stood up, went to the tent's opening and looked outside. The sky had cleared. The rain was over for now. Huge white clouds were banked in rising tiers like gigantic puffs of cotton wool.

I felt shaken, and years older. And I had a powerful feeling that Saba was standing right beside me.

You don't even know that she was your mother, do you? I thought. *But you ought to. She must have loved you best, because you were the one she took. If she'd taken me, I'd have been wherever you are, and you'd be standing right here, in this lousy tent.*

And I called out softly, 'Where are you, Saba? Where?'

CHAPTER TWENTY-THREE

Tariq came home late.

'What's up with all these earthworks?' he said.

'It's a trench we dug to keep out the rainwater,' I said.

'Good idea! I was scared we'd get flooded out. What a storm! I got soaked, splashing around with water bottles in all that rain. What's for supper, Safiya? I'm starving.'

'Aubergine and peppers in tomato sauce. Listen, I want to talk to you.'

'Not now. Go away. I've got to change.'

When I came out of my room, Tariq was towelling his thick black hair, making it stand up in spikes.

I spooned his supper out on to his plate.

'What did you want to ask me, then?' he said, dipping his bread into the sauce.

'Malik told me something today, about Mama. She didn't die when Saba and I were born, but she got ill.'

His hand stopped mid-air, halfway to his mouth.

'*What?* What are you talking about? Of course she died! You know she did!'

'No, honestly, Tariq. Malik told me. She had a mental illness.'

He'd gone a funny colour.

'You don't mean – Safiya, she's not still alive?'

I shook my head.

'No. I thought that at first. But she's not. She took Saba to Amman and died there.'

'This is so weird! How come no one ever told us? Why didn't she take me?' He broke off angrily.

'Well, she didn't take me either.'

Tariq had lost interest in his supper. He pushed his plate away.

'How awful for Baba!' he said.

I felt ashamed. I'd only been thinking about myself. I hadn't thought about Tariq or Baba at all.

'So how did she die?' he went on.

'Malik doesn't know.'

'I mean, mental illness doesn't kill you. Unless – *wallah*, Safiya, she didn't kill herself, did she?'

A shiver went down my spine.

'I told you! Malik couldn't tell me! And you know what, Tariq, I'm sick of all the secrets in this family. I think we should be told the truth.'

He thought about this for a moment.

'I agree,' he said at last. 'I'll wait till there's a good moment, then I'll ask Baba. It's not fair to keep us in the dark.' He frowned. 'You're sure you got all that right, Safiya? It's so – it's just incredible! Mama, having a mental illness and taking Saba away herself. And nobody even told us!'

I nodded.

'Ask Malik yourself if you don't believe me.'

I watched Tariq as at last he ate his supper. His hair had grown long because he'd never had time to get it cut. I saw him only early in the morning, when I dragged myself out of bed to get his breakfast ready, and then again in the evening, when he almost fell into the tent, dog tired and hungry, gobbling his supper before he forced himself to study. On Fridays and Saturdays, when there was no school, he put in double time at the bottling plant, then worked furiously at home.

I'd been so busy with my own worries I hadn't thought about how tough life was for him.

He leaned forward and gave my arm a squeeze.

'I can't take it all in, Safiya. It's all too weird. Poor old Baba. No wonder he couldn't bear to tell us. He's had a sad life, hasn't he? We've got to really look after him now.'

I wasn't sure I liked this new Tariq. Where was my annoying brother, the one I'd always played with and fought with? This Tariq was like a grown-up.

He's left me behind, I thought.

CHAPTER TWENTY-FOUR

I lay in bed the following morning thinking of secrets. Our family was full of them. How had Mama died? Why had she taken Saba and not me? Why had Uncle Hassan and his family disappeared from our lives? And, most important of all, where was Saba now?

I'm going to find you, I thought. *And nobody's going to stop me.*

But how do you find a person who doesn't even know you exist? Whose 'parents' don't want you to find her? Who could be in America, or Amman, or on the moon, for all I knew. And how do you start when you haven't even got a phone, and you're stuck in a tent day after day, and the only place you ever go to is the house next door and the shop a few metres away?

Think positively, Safiya, I told myself sternly. *There are two clues to follow up. One is to ask Baba about what happened to Mama.*

That idea made me nervous. I hated the thought of upsetting him.

The other, I went on, *is to catch Uncle Yasser on his own again and find out if he really did see Uncle Hassan in Amman.*

*

My chance with Uncle Yasser came sooner than I'd expected, because he came round in the middle of the morning, squelching his way through the puddles to get into the tent.

'I came by to see if you were all right,' he said, 'what with the rain and everything. You dug a trench! Good idea. Got a spade, have you?'

Malik had retreated into his usual shy silence, but now he found his voice.

'I just – I used a bit of old tent pole.'

Uncle Yasser looked impressed.

'You dug a trench all the way round the tent with an old pole?'

Malik flushed.

'We – I had to. The water was coming in.'

'I'll get you a spade,' Uncle Yasser said, looking at Malik with new respect. 'You'll need to make it deeper before the next storm comes.'

Malik was still wearing Baba's old clothes. He smiled, and for a strange, dizzying moment he looked just like his older brother.

'Thank you, Abu Fares,' he said. 'That would be very helpful.'

Uncle Yasser was still studying him, as if he was trying to make up his mind.

'Have you found work yet?'

Malik should his head.

'No, sir. It's hard. No one here knows me. There are so many Syrian men like me, out of work and looking for jobs.'

'But you've done building work before, haven't you?'

'Yes!' Malik leaned forward eagerly. 'Bricklaying, carpentry, plastering, electrical . . .'

Uncle Yasser clapped him on the shoulder.

'Well then, come to the bottling plant with me now. The storm dislodged something in my roof and the rain's coming in. Is that something you could fix?'

'Oh yes!' Malik's face lit up. 'I – I just need to change into my work clothes.'

Uncle Yasser and I went outside to give him space. My heart gave a kick. This was my chance!

'Uncle Yasser,' I said, plucking up my courage, 'can I ask you something?'

He was looking at his watch.

'Yes, of course. What is it?'

'I – I heard Aunt Zainab say that you'd seen my uncle, Hassan, in Amman. Did you?'

He looked surprised.

'Hassan? Yes, months ago. He was going into that big engineering company's headquarters. Askil International, I think it's called. I might have been wrong. It was only a glimpse.'

Askil International! It must have been him! I thought triumphantly.

'Was there anyone with him? A – a girl?'

'What? No, he was on his own. But I couldn't be sure it was him. It could have been anybody.'

'Thank you, dear Uncle!' I said, and I surprised us both by darting forward and kissing him on the cheek.

CHAPTER TWENTY-FIVE

I was alone in the tent that afternoon, washing out Snowball's bowl, when a rattling of the compound gate sent my heart thudding. Someone was trying to get in. It couldn't be Baba. He was still in Zarka. Tariq was at school and Malik was with Uncle Yasser. I was so frightened that I sat frozen, not daring to move. All Baba's warnings flashed through my mind. At any minute I might face a thief, a kidnapper, or . . .

As the gate swung open, I made a dive for my cubicle and started burrowing under my blanket to hide myself.

Then I heard Baba's voice.

'Safiya! I saw you! What are you doing? Come out of there! Why are you here on your own?'

'Baba!' I crawled out of my cubicle, feeling silly. 'I didn't expect you back till later. Uncle Malik's gone out with Uncle Yasser. They only left a few minutes ago.'

He took off his jacket and sat down on his mattress.

'Can I get you some tea?' I asked him. 'Something to eat?'

'That's my lovely girl,' he said. 'Being kind to your old Baba, eh?'

I watched him out of the corner of my eye as I made his tea. He seemed to be in a good mood, and no one would come in to interrupt us for hours.

'Baba,' I said, as gently as I could, handing him the tea glass and sitting down beside him on the mattress, 'Uncle Malik told me something yesterday, about – about Mama.'

'Oh yes? What did he say?' He sounded defensive.

'He said she didn't die when I – we – were born, but she got ill afterwards and went off to Amman with Saba. Can you – could you tell me how it happened?'

He frowned.

'Malik had no business to . . .' Then he caught my eye and the old, sad look settled on his face.

'Well, I suppose you're old enough to know the truth. My poor Mariam! She had a very difficult birth with the two of you. Then she was – she had – a severe depression. Nobody realized how bad it was. We thought she just needed to rest. She should have had help! She would have got better completely in a few weeks with the right care. But I was in trouble myself. The *mukhabarat* were already watching me. She was worried I might be arrested, and it quickly turned into paranoia. I blame myself!' He shook his head wearily. 'I should have done more to help her! It was all my fault!'

'I'm sorry, Baba,' I said in a small voice. 'I didn't want to upset you. It's just that I needed to know. *We* needed to know.'

He didn't seem to have heard me.

'It got worse,' he went on. 'She started being terrified of everything and everybody. She was even afraid of me! "I must go home!" she kept saying. "I've got to go to Jordan! The *mukhabarat* will get me here. I need my brother to protect me!"'

I was clenching my hands so tightly that my nails were digging into my palms.

'Did you take her to Amman yourself, Baba? She didn't go alone, did she?'

'I was at the office, *habibti*. I would have stopped her if I'd known what she was going to do. Shirin was at home with her. "I've got an appointment with the doctor," Mariam told her. "Look after the children for an hour or two." Shirin didn't suspect anything. Saba started crying. Mariam picked her up and rocked her, but Saba wouldn't settle. Then she heard a car horn in the street. "That's my taxi," she said. "I'll take Saba with me," and she grabbed her bag and ran out of the house.'

'Why didn't she take me too, Baba?' I blurted out. 'And Tariq? Was it because she didn't – didn't love us?'

He put his arm round me and pulled me close.

'Of course she loved you, Safiya! She adored all three of you. She didn't plan to take Saba and leave you behind. If you'd been the one who was crying, she'd have taken you instead. She wasn't herself. She was – she must have been – just terribly afraid.'

A little voice in my head said, *I don't believe you. It wasn't like that. She loved Saba. She didn't love me.*

Baba was looking out through the tent opening, lost in his own thoughts. I nudged him.

'What happened then? Go on, Baba.'

'I got a phone call from Shirin. "Mariam's gone out," she said. "She told me she was going to the doctor, but I called the surgery and she didn't show up." I rushed home at once, went into our bedroom and found her bedside drawer open. Her passport had gone. I guessed then. She must have left the country, hired a car to drive her across the border into Jordan, to Amman, to her brother.'

'With Saba.'

'Yes, with Saba.'

'What did you do?'

'I tried again and again to call Hassan. I was frantic! It was evening before I could get hold of him. He told me she'd just arrived and that she was in such a state he'd locked her in her bedroom and given her a sedative. "Don't come, Adnan," he kept saying. "She's terrified of you. What have you done to my sister?"'

'That's ridiculous!' I said indignantly.

'I couldn't have gone, anyway. I wouldn't have been allowed out of the country. I called every hour, day after day, begging to speak to her. Pleading with Hassan to send her back to me. She wouldn't talk to me. "You're making things worse," Hassan kept saying. "Give her time. She just needs to rest, Adnan. Leave her alone for a bit. The baby's crying a lot. She's got a small blockage inside but we've got the best doctor in Amman to sort it out. She can't be moved at the moment. Israa adores her, don't worry. Mariam'll be better soon . . .'" He stopped.

'But she didn't get better, did she? Go on, Baba!'

'Why didn't I make her see a psychiatrist?' He hit himself on the chest with his fist. 'I ask myself that all the time. Perhaps I could have slipped across the border somehow, gone to Amman . . . But you were newborn too! And there was Tariq! How could I have left you?'

I couldn't think of anything to say.

'Her paranoia got even worse in Amman,' he went on. 'She was even afraid of Hassan. He didn't tell me! He just kept sending me reassuring messages – she was fine, the baby was fine, she was resting, no she didn't want me to come. Then one day she ran out into the street in a panic. There was a van . . .'

We sat in silence for a moment.

I was shuddering inside, imagining the terrible moment, hearing the screech of tyres, the shouts and the sickening crash. I was too shocked to cry. All I could do was grab Baba's arm and hold it as tight as I could until the shaking stopped.

He sighed one more time, then smiled weakly. He tugged his arm out of my grip, put it round my shoulders and pulled me close.

'You know what, Safiya, I'm glad we've had this talk. It's time you knew the truth. But people are funny about mental illness. They think it's shameful. I'll talk to Tariq about it tonight, but, after that, better to keep it to ourselves, eh?'

'That's so unfair!' I burst out. 'She was sick, not crazy. If she'd had the right treatment, she'd have got better and we'd all still be together, and Saba would be here with us, and . . .'

'I know, *habibti*, but that's just the way it is. I've lived with it all these years. The pain doesn't go away, but I'm used to it now. And we still have each other, after all.'

Yes, I thought, *but we should have Saba too.*

CHAPTER TWENTY-SIX

I dreamed again that night. I was in the kind of tent made of black woven goats' hair that our Syrian ancestors had lived in a long time ago. Soft rugs, glowing with jewel-like colours, covered the floor and tasselled cushions lined the edges. There was a fireplace in the centre built up on hearthstones, and beside it was a huge round brass tray. Elegant coffee pots with long curved spouts were lined up like a row of soldiers.

The dream changed. Now I was in a garden beside the tent. There were trees and flowers, fountains and cushioned benches shaded by vines.

Saba was there. She was feeding a bird with a long blue tail, which was perched on her wrist. I tried to run towards her, but something was tangled round my feet. I opened my mouth, but no sound came out. A woman in a familiar long white wedding dress appeared.

She beckoned to Saba.

'Coming, Mama,' said Saba, and she followed the woman through a doorway and out of sight.

'No!' I tried to shout. 'Don't go! Don't you know me? Take me with you!'

Then I woke up. I was in my damp bed, the smell of mouldy canvas in my nostrils. I'd been thrashing about in my sleep. My blanket had slipped off, and I was cold. Baba was already up. I could hear him coughing. It was time to start the day.

CHAPTER TWENTY-SEVEN

'You must go to your aunt today,' Baba said as I got the breakfast ready. 'I'll be out till this afternoon.'

It had been several days since I'd been at the house. I braced myself to face Aunt Zainab as I brushed specks of dried mud off my coat. There was no point in doing anything about my muddy shoes. They'd get dirty again as soon as I stepped outside. Anyway, hers would be just as bad.

I heard voices inside as I knocked on the door. Aunt Zainab took a while to open it.

'Oh, it's you,' she said. 'What do you want?'

'Baba's out today, Aunt. He asked if I could be with you.'

'Well, you can't.' She turned away. 'I'm going out with my sister. You can't stay in the house on your own.'

'Who is it?' called out Um Salim, coming out of the kitchen. '*Kifek halik, habibti?* How are you?'

'Very well, thank you.' The sight of her kind face was as good as a hug.

'And how did you manage in all that rain?' she went on. 'I thought of you in that tent, you know.'

'They were perfectly all right,' Aunt Zainab broke in scornfully. 'Yasser made quite sure the tent was a good one. The way he fusses over you all . . .'

'We were fine, Um Salim, thank you. Uncle Yasser is very kind,' I said, avoiding Aunt Zainab's glare.

A car horn sounded outside.

'The taxi's here already,' said Aunt Zainab. 'I'm sorry, Safiya, but you'll have to go back to the tent. Just stay inside and don't open the gate.'

Behind her, Um Salim was frowning.

'A bit risky, isn't it, Zainab? A young girl on her own? Why don't we take her with us?'

My heart leaped with excitement. It had been so long since I'd been anywhere that the thought of an expedition, however small, was thrilling.

'Oh, but that's . . .' began Aunt Zainab.

'Think about it.' Her sister was smiling at me. 'I'm sure Safiya knows how to make herself useful. She can help with carrying the bags if we get time to go to the market. Anyway, the poor child must be fearfully bored, stuck around here all day with nothing to do.'

Nothing to do, eh? I thought. *Only mountains of clothes to wash, all the meals to cook and endless mud to sweep out of the tent.*

Aunt Zainab shrugged.

'Well, I suppose so. But for heaven's sake, Safiya, go and retie that hijab. It's all over the place.'

'Sorry, Aunt.' I flushed with embarrassment. 'There's

no mirror in the tent. I . . .'

'Come here, *habibti,*' said Um Salim. 'Let me do it for you.'

Aunt Zainab was patting her pockets.

'Where's my phone?' she said. She went back into the house to look for it.

Um Salim untied my hijab, smoothed my hair back and retied it. The feel of her soft hands fluttering around my head was so lovely that I almost wanted to cry.

Behind us we could hear Aunt Zainab clattering around, looking for her phone.

'You're a pretty girl,' said Um Salim, studying my face with her head on one side. 'You should look after your skin. Use moisturizers.'

My hand flew involuntarily to hide my teeth.

'Oh that!' she laughed. 'You'll get braces to correct them one of these days.'

Moisturizer? Braces? I thought. *You must be joking, Um Salim. We can hardly afford to eat.*

Aloud, I said, 'Where are we going?'

She looked surprised.

'Didn't Zainab tell you? Our niece is getting married. There are parties every day this week. We're getting facial treatments done today. We've already had our hair roots seen to, nails lacquered . . .' She held her hands out to me, palms down. 'Do you like this shade of pink?'

Before I could answer, Aunt Zainab was back.

'Under a tea towel in the kitchen,' she snapped at her

sister. 'You might have been more careful. You were the one doing the drying up.'

She locked the door behind us and swept out to the taxi. Um Salim winked at me behind her back.

'Don't take any notice,' she whispered. 'Her bark is much worse than her bite.'

CHAPTER TWENTY-EIGHT

Aunt Zainab made me sit in front of the taxi beside the driver while she and Um Salim sat in the back and gossiped about their niece.

'I'm surprised they found anyone to marry that girl,' Aunt Zainab said. 'The way she carries on! Gave the whole family a bad reputation.'

'She's just high-spirited,' Um Salim said. 'She'll settle down once she's married.'

Those sisters! One was like a cough drop, the other like a chocolate.

As soon as we were off the bumpy track and on the tarmac road into town, I stopped listening to them. I'd been stuck moving between our tent and Uncle Yasser's house for so long that everything looked interesting, even the sight of two ragged little girls playing a clapping game outside a makeshift shack. Were they refugees from Syria? I longed to stop and talk to them.

I looked eagerly at the shops we passed: a hardware store with coloured plastic bowls piled up outside, a toyshop with dolls wrapped in glittering cellophane, a patisserie with piles of cakes and pastries in the window.

I was like a thirsty person drinking my first glass of water at the end of a long, hot day.

We'd only gone about a mile when I spotted Uncle Yasser's truck. It was parked outside a large building with big double doors open at the front. A man was running out, holding heavy water bottles by their handles, one in each hand. He heaved them up on to the back of the truck then ran back inside for more.

So this was Uncle Yasser's water bottling plant! The taxi had slowed down behind a bus that had stopped to pick up passengers. I tried to see into the gloomy space beyond the yawning entrance, but all I could make out was the glint of steel pipes and the blue gleam from stacks of water bottles. The man ran out again with two more heavy loads.

This must be what Tariq did all the time! I could see why he got so exhausted.

Aunt Zainab leaned over Um Salim to point something out to her.

'See that guttering hanging down? Storm damage. The place eats up money.'

Malik! He must be up there somewhere, working on repairs. I craned my neck to look, but the taxi was overtaking a big truck that blocked my view.

A few minutes later, we were in the centre of town. There wasn't much to see. Azraq was a small place, with low-rise buildings set back behind rough unpaved forecourts beside the busy main road. Heavy trucks were pulled up off the edge of the tarmac, and others rumbled down the main street. Everything was a dull brown colour, layered with the gritty dust that blew in whenever the wind was strong. Now the rain had turned the dust to mud.

The taxi driver pulled up in a side street, and we got out.

'Don't dawdle, Safiya,' Aunt Zainab said over her shoulder, pushing open a glass door on which was stencilled a picture of a woman with flowing blonde hair, pouting scarlet lips and eyelashes sticking out a mile. *Perfumes of Paradise, Beauty Salon* was written underneath in curly, frosted writing.

I followed the sisters up a narrow staircase into the little reception area, and was half knocked out by the heady scent of cosmetics and perfume.

'Safiya! Don't just stand there! Come in properly and shut the door behind you,' barked Aunt Zainab.

A woman with a cloud of thick, curled hair was coming out through a bead curtain.

'Ladies! Welcome.' She turned to me. 'And has this young lady come for a treatment too?'

'No.' Aunt Zainab took off her hijab and shook out her own hair. 'Safiya, sit there, and don't get in Um Khalid's way.'

She pointed to a chair by the door. The beautician's eyes swept past me as if I didn't exist.

She thinks I'm a servant, I thought, clenching my fists on my lap.

Um Khalid held open the door to the treatment room.

'It's facials today, isn't it? Come through. Fatima is ready for you.'

The door shut behind them and I was alone. There was a pile of magazines on a low table beside me. In Damascus, we used to swap our favourite magazines at school. Auntie Shirin thought they were silly and had never let me buy them. Sometimes, though, I'd managed to borrow one and sneak it home to read. I'd loved the gossip about my favourite film stars.

I was soon so engrossed that I didn't hear Um Khalid coming back, but as she started fussing around her desk, tutting with annoyance, I looked up.

'Where is it?' she was muttering. 'I had it a minute ago.'

A paper had fallen on to the floor. I darted forward to pick it up.

'Is this what you're looking for?' I said.

She looked surprised.

'You're educated? I saw you looking at that magazine. You can read?'

I flushed.

'Yes. Of course.'

'You're not their servant, then?'

'Abu Fares is my father's cousin.' I said stiffly.

'Ah!' Her face cleared. 'The lawyer from Damascus!'

That put me on my guard. What had she heard about

us from Aunt Zainab? Nothing good, I was sure. But she
was smiling.

'People say he's a good man. One day, *inshallah*, all this
trouble will be over.'

As she turned back to the desk, the loose sleeve of her
robe caught on a pile of papers and swept them on to the
floor.

'There I go again!' she said, exasperated. 'Everything's
gone wrong today. My laptop's given up on me, and I've
got to do all this paperwork by hand. If there's one thing
I hate, it's sorting out figures.'

Her mobile buzzed.

'Yes, of course, Abu Mohammed,' she said in a syrupy
voice. 'Your invoice will be settled today. No, really. I
promise.'

She put the phone down and started picking up one
piece of paper after another as if she was despairing of
getting them in order.

'Would you like me to help you?' I asked impulsively.

'You?' she looked surprised. 'But you're only – how
old are you?'

'Nearly thirteen. I – I was top of the class in maths at
school.'

She looked at me doubtfully.

'But I don't know you! What if you make mistakes?'

I flushed.

'No. Of course. I'm sorry. It was cheeky of me. It's
just that I've always loved working with figures.'

Her phone rang again.

'Yes, sir. Of course. Today!' She rolled her eyes at me. 'My – my assistant is working on the accounts now.'

She put the phone down.

'What did you say your name was?'

I shivered with excitement.

'Safiya.'

'Well, Safiya, you've got yourself a job. Take off your coat and sit down here, at the desk.'

She plunged into a load of explanations, then went off and left me to it.

I sat frozen in panic. What if I screwed it all up?

Come on, Safiya, I told myself. *You were top in maths, remember?*

Once I'd got started, it was easy. I loved making my brain work again. The room was deliciously warm, and there was even music from some of my favourite films. I hadn't heard any music for ages and hadn't known how much I'd missed it.

I'd just finished adding up a long column of figures when Aunt Zainab and Um Salim came out of the beauty room. Aunt Zainab stopped dead when she saw me sitting at Um Khalid's desk, a fresh glass of mint tea beside me.

'Safiya! What *do* you think you're doing?'

Um Khalid fluttered out behind her.

'Oh, Safiya's wonderful!' she gushed. 'You've no idea how grateful I am. My accounts are nearly done already! She must come again tomorrow. I'll send a taxi for her.

There's a whole backlog of stuff that needs dealing with.'

I watched Aunt Zainab's face, holding my breath.

'It's out of the quest—' she began.

'Why not?' interrupted Um Salim. 'If she's making herself useful, of course she should come.'

'That's settled, then.' Um Khalid looked out of the window. 'Your taxi's here. Till tomorrow, Safiya. So lucky that you came today.'

I danced out to the taxi feeling like a prisoner whose cell door had been thrown open.

'You didn't lose any time pushing yourself forward,' said Aunt Zainab disapprovingly as the taxi overtook a convoy of military vehicles. 'I hope you didn't make a nuisance of yourself. Um Khalid's got a soft heart. People take advantage.'

But her voice had lost its usual sting. I stared boldly back at her in the car mirror.

'I *wasn't* a nuisance, Aunt. Her laptop's broken. She hadn't paid her suppliers for weeks. People kept phoning up about their invoices not being settled.'

Aunt Zainab grunted as if she was unconvinced, but before she looked away I saw in her eyes a flash of something that might have been respect.

CHAPTER TWENTY-NINE

Baba was home when I got back to the tent. He sniffed at me suspiciously.

'Where have you been? You're not wearing perfume, are you?'

He was going to need careful handling, I could tell.

'Aunt Zainab and her sister took me to the beauty parlour in Azraq. They go there all the time.'

You can't object to that, I thought.

'Well, if you were with them . . .'

'I was. The owner, Um Khalid, she's really nice, Baba. All her accounts and stuff were in a muddle and I helped to sort them for her.'

He was losing interest. I raised my voice, willing him to look at me. 'I loved going there, Baba. I haven't been anywhere at all since we came to Jordan and that was months ago. It's so boring, stuck here all the time. Even just going to Azraq was a treat.'

He looked startled.

'Well, yes, I see. I'm sorry, *habibti*. I hadn't realized. We'll just have to hope that your aunt takes you out again.'

He got out his phone. I had to pull him back.

'The thing is, Baba, Um Khalid was really grateful. She wants me to go back tomorrow and help her do an inventory of all her stuff.'

'With your aunt?'

'N-no. On my own. She said she'd send a taxi for me.'

He was shaking his head before I'd finished speaking.

'Now, Safiya, you know that's quite out of the question. Let you go in a taxi, to a place I don't know, to a woman I've never met? What are you thinking of?'

I stood my ground.

'There's nothing bad about Um Khalid. Ask Aunt Zainab. She goes there all the time.'

'Then get her to take you with her next time she goes! You must see that I can't possibly let you go on your own.'

'Baba!' I had crossed my arms over my chest, but was afraid I looked aggressive, so I dropped them again. 'Listen, please! Aunt Zainab won't take me if she can help it. She doesn't like me one bit. She only let me go because her sister persuaded her to.'

'If Zainab didn't want you to go again, she probably knows it's not a respectable place. That's enough, Safiya. Stop this now.'

'If you could only ask her yourself!' I pleaded. 'Don't you see? I'm trapped here, all day, every day. It was so great today. I actually used my brain. It was like being back at school. Don't just leave me here to rot, Baba. Please!'

He didn't answer at once. I held my breath. At last he

sighed and said, 'It is hard for you, I know. All right. I'll speak to Zainab.'

He picked up his briefcase and began to open it. I didn't move.

'What's the matter now?' He was starting to look angry. I dropped down to sit beside him.

'Baba, Aunt Zainab's at home and Um Salim – that's her sister – is with her. You – you could ask them straight away. Aunt Zainab's much more likely to be helpful if Um Salim's still there.'

To my relief he laughed, half amused, half exasperated.

'You don't give up, do you? All right, Safiya. But you stay here. I don't want you hovering around me while I hear what the pair of them have to say.'

It seemed like ages before Baba came back. I was tempted to creep up to the house and listen outside the door, but the thought of being caught was too horrible.

'That sister of Zainab's is a very charming woman,' he said, coming back at last and shuffling off his shoes at the entrance to the tent. 'She likes you, *habibti*.' He patted my arm. 'And so she should.'

'Yes, Baba, but what about . . .'

'This beautician woman? Um Salim was at school with her. A respectable family. The husband has a business in Zarka.'

'So does that mean I can . . .'

He nodded.

'I don't see any harm in it.'

I flew at him, flung my arms round him and hugged him tight.

'But –' he gently pushed me away – 'I need to meet her first to see for myself. And as for going on your own in a taxi, that's impossible.'

I opened my mouth to protest, but shut it again. I'd won one battle. The next one could wait.

'So can we go tomorrow, Baba? She wants me there in the morning.'

'All right, *habibti*. And no need for a taxi. It's only a mile or so into town. We'll walk.'

CHAPTER THIRTY

I didn't sleep well that night, and by the time I woke up my confidence had oozed away. I looked all wrong for a beauty salon. My clothes were nearly worn out, my fingernails were chipped and my hands were red with doing the washing in cold water. Even kind Um Salim had noticed my bad skin and my sticking-out teeth.

Um Khalid wants you for your brains, not your looks, I told myself. *Stop worrying. There's nothing you can do about it, anyway.*

Baba ate his breakfast without saying a word about Perfumes of Paradise.

He's forgotten, I thought anxiously.

I started sweeping the floor around him, making myself as obvious as possible.

At last he looked up.

'Stop buzzing around me like a fly. It's not even eight o'clock. Your precious salon won't open till nine at the earliest.'

'Oh!' I laughed, embarrassed. 'Sorry, Baba. It's just that I . . .'

'You thought I'd forgotten. Well, I haven't. We'll go

when I've finished reading this newspaper. And, Safiya – '
he looked at me over his reading glasses, his face suddenly
stern. 'I've been very indulgent with you. Not many
fathers would let their daughters talk back to them the
way you talk to me. Don't push me too far.'

It was wonderful walking out with Baba, even though it
was only along the dreary road into Azraq. Back home,
we'd often gone to a pastry shop at the weekend. I'd
spend ages choosing cakes from the glass-fronted display
case, then watch as the sales assistant slid them into a box
and tied it with fancy string.

Do you remember, I wanted to ask Baba, *how the pastry-
shop man used to wobble when he laughed?* But I didn't.
Memories of home always made us sad.

It was too late to ask him, anyway. He'd already pushed
open the door and was halfway up the stairs.

Um Khalid clapped her hands as she came out through
the bead curtain and saw me.

'Safiya! *Alhamdulillah!* Thank God you came back.
And this is . . .'

'My father, Abu Tariq. He wants to check . . . I mean,
to see . . .'

'Of course.' She nodded approvingly. 'I'm glad you
came.' She pushed her head through the bead curtain.
'Fatima! Tea for our guest!'

Baba sat down on a spindly gilt chair. He looked as out
of place as a cactus in a bouquet of roses.

I watched admiringly as Um Khalid twisted him round her little finger. She was businesslike, but she knew how to flatter him too. Within twenty minutes, Baba had agreed to let me come to the salon as often as I was needed, had been shown the work Um Khalid wanted me to do and had said I could probably manage it.

'There's just the question of . . .' he began, getting up to go.

'I'm glad you brought it up!' Um Khalid interrupted. 'One JD for every day she works here. And I'd give her lunch, of course. I wish it could be more, but . . .'

My heart leapt. I'd actually be paid!

But Baba was frowning.

'It's the question of transport. I can't allow Safiya . . .'

'No, no, you're right.' Once again, Um Khalid had jumped ahead of him. She picked up her phone, keyed in a number and murmured into the receiver.

A moment later, heavy footsteps plodded up the stairs and a stout old man stood wheezing in the doorway.

'This is my uncle, Abu Tewfik,' Um Khalid said. 'He has a taxi and runs all my client calls from his office downstairs.'

Baba smiled politely, but looked doubtful.

'Thank you. We'll see how it goes. For today, I'll come back myself to fetch Safiya.'

I could read his mind as easily as if he'd spoken.

You're going to check up on him, I thought.

My eyes met Um Khalid's. She hid a smile. She'd understood perfectly.

I struggled a bit that first full day at Perfumes of Paradise. I'd impressed Um Khalid too much and she expected miracles. But once the clients started arriving, and she was working in the beauty room, I could sort things out on my own.

The phone rang soon after I'd started. Yesterday, Um Khalid had always run out to answer it, but now a hair dryer was humming loudly in the beauty room and she couldn't hear it ring. Was I supposed to answer it or not? I waited a bit, then I picked it up.

'Perfumes of Paradise,' I said, putting on a grown-up voice. '*Sabah alkheer.* To whom am I speaking? No, Um Khalid is engaged with a client. Shall I ask her to call you back? Yes, do give me your name again. I'll make a note of it.'

'Who was that?' said Um Khalid, jangling the beads as she came through the curtain.

'Someone called Um Nasser.'

'That woman! She's impossible. I heard you just now, Safiya. You did well. You'd better go on dealing with calls.'

The day sped past. I kept finding more bits of paper that needed sorting out, and clients called all the time. I was surprised when Um Khalid glanced out of the window and said, 'Here's your father. Can you be here by nine tomorrow? And I don't mean to criticize, but do you have a – well – a prettier hijab?'

I went scarlet.

'No. I . . .'

She reached into the drawer of her desk and pulled out a white scarf printed with pale blue flowers.

'This should suit you. I'll show you tomorrow how to tie it more fashionably, with a pearl pin.'

By the end of the week, I felt as if I'd been at the salon forever. I loved it. Baba had decided to trust Abu Tewfik, who picked me up every morning at nine and dropped me back at five. He never said much, but he had a way of groaning as he got in and out of the car that worried me at first.

'Indigestion,' he said on the second day, having caught my eye in the mirror.

That was a relief. I was afraid I'd been annoying him.

I was busy all the time. Apart from the accounts, I had to tidy the shelves (they'd got into an awful mess), sort out the laundry and answer the phone. I was really tired when I got home, but then I had to cook the supper. Baba tried to help. He even swept out the tent once, but he did it so badly I had to do it again.

I didn't mind working hard. In fact, I liked it. And there was an extra JD in my pocket at the end of each day, money that I'd earned myself.

I kept thinking about Um Khalid's laptop.

The minute I get my hands on it, I'll search for Askil International! I told Saba in my head. *There's sure to be a phone number for the office in Amman. Don't worry! I'm coming!*

The laptop was delivered back to the salon a few days later. Um Khalid handed it to me.

'You do know how to use this, don't you?' she said.

'Yes, of course!'

It wasn't really a lie. We'd had IT lessons at school and I'd often played around on Tariq's old laptop.

'Good,' she said. 'I keep forgetting you're only four-teen.'

Not quite thirteen, I nearly said, but then my eye fell on the desktop calendar. My birthday had been two weeks ago! I'd forgotten it, and so had everyone else.

Before I could start feeling sorry for myself, Um Khalid looked at her watch and said, 'Time for you to go now, dear. Abu Tewfik will be waiting. Don't be late tomorrow. We're going to be busy. Appointments end to end.'

CHAPTER THIRTY-ONE

The next morning, I woke with a cramping pain in my stomach. I felt scared. Was I ill?

I got up and gasped with fright. There was blood between my legs and on my nightdress.

'Baba!' I called out, trying not to panic. 'I'm bleeding!'

He pulled aside the canvas flap, letting more light into my cubicle, looked down, then quickly looked away. He'd gone red with embarrassment.

'Shh!' he said, looking over his shoulder. 'You don't want Malik and Tariq to hear.'

'What? Why not? Baba . . .'

'It's only . . . It's something normal.'

'*Normal?* I'm *bleeding*! It's really serious!'

'Don't worry about it,' he said. 'Stay there. I'll fetch Zainab. She can help – fix you up . . .'

He dropped the flap and a moment later I heard the gate clang. I waited, while waves of pain came and went. Had I done something wrong? Would Aunt Zainab be angry?

Tariq and Malik had gone off with Uncle Yasser before Baba came back with Aunt Zainab. She laughed when she saw my face.

'You look as if you've seen a ghost, dear.' It was the first time she'd called me 'dear'. I found that scary, to be honest. 'Don't you know what this is? It's never happened before?'

'No,' I whispered. 'Is it serious, Aunt? Will I have to go to hospital?'

She laughed again.

'Hospital? Of course not! It's only your monthlies. It means you're growing up, that's all. Didn't that snooty aunt of yours explain? It's what happens to every woman, every month. Put your coat on over that nightdress and come to the house. You can clean up in the bathroom and I'll give you what you need to cope with the bleeding. You have to soak the bloodstains in cold water. It's the only way to get them out.'

'Th-thank you, Aunt,' I said, and I meant it. Somehow, her no-nonsense approach was more reassuring than too much sympathy.

As I bent to pick up my coat, another cramp came.

'Could you call Um Khalid, Aunt,' I said, 'and tell her I can't come to the salon today?'

Her eyebrows shot up.

'Not go? Why ever not? Look, Safiya, this is something normal. You have to deal with it. And do it privately. No one likes talking about it.' Then she wagged a finger at me. 'You need to be careful now, my girl. There'll be other changes happening to you. To your shape. Men will start looking at you in a different way. Your reputation is a sacred thing. Once you lose it, you can never get it back, and the whole family suffers.'

I hardly heard her. Another wave of pain had hit me.

'I'll give you something for the cramps.' She sounded almost sympathetic. 'Come on. Abu Tewfik will be here in under an hour. You can't let Um Khalid down.' She hesitated. 'I must say, Safiya, I'm impressed by the way you've wormed your way into her good graces.' She saw me flinch, and tossed her head impatiently. 'Oh, don't take offence. I didn't mean it like that. You've done well. I didn't know you had it in you. Um Khalid tells me you're really quite useful.'

CHAPTER THIRTY-TWO

An hour later, I was in the taxi. A painkiller had lessened the cramps and now that I was over the shock I was almost excited. It felt as if I'd joined a secret society whose private language every woman understood. But then a wave of loneliness washed over me and I had to swallow tears.

If only you'd been with me today, Mama, I thought. *You'd have explained everything properly, and hugged away the pain. And Saba – did it start for you today too? I don't see why it's all got to be such a secret. It happens to every girl, after all.*

I almost expected Um Khalid to see the change in me, but she only glanced up, said, '*Kifek,* Safiya?' and went on frowning at her phone.

The laptop was on the desk. Its shiny top gleamed enticingly. I sat down, switched it on and typed in the password Um Khalid had written out for me, then watched impatiently as it slowly booted up. My eyes flew to the internet icon. It wasn't connecting!

Um Khalid leaned over me and typed in the internet password. I watched as carefully as I could but couldn't make out what it was. She brought up the salon's emails.

'Go through the inbox,' she said. 'Delete the adverts and make a note of anything that looks urgent.'

Then she tapped me on the shoulder.

'No straying now. I know what you girls are like on the internet. No social media, no searching for your friends! Get on with it.'

A stout, breathless woman came puffing up the stairs into the reception room. Um Khalid darted out from behind the desk.

'*Ahlan wa sahlan ya, habibti!*' she gushed, kissing her on both cheeks. 'Come into the beauty room. Fatima is waiting for you.'

A moment later, I was alone. Holding my breath, I typed 'Askil International' into the search line. I hadn't even clicked on it when Um Khalid burst back through the bead curtain. My heart thudding, I managed just in time to flick back to the email screen.

'Good,' she said, pulling the laptop round to look at the screen. 'You've got into the account. I thought you might need another password.' She took her coat off the peg behind the door. 'I have to go out now. I'll be back in half an hour.'

I waited a full five minutes after she'd gone, then could bear it no longer and feverishly typed 'Askil International Amman' into the search bar again. A few seconds later, I had scribbled a phone number and an address on a piece of paper and had tucked it into my pocket.

The phone beside me buzzed. I picked it up, but the

caller rang off. The phone was still in my hand. Before I knew what I was doing, I'd tapped in the number of Askil International. The call went through at once. A posh receptionist's voice said breathily, 'Askil International. *Na'am?*'

Panic! I wasn't ready! I hadn't thought out what to say!

'Um, *salaam alaikum*,' I began feebly.

'Yes? Can I help you?'

I took a deep breath.

'I'm – I'm making enquiries about one of your employees. Mr Hassan Ahmed. I believe he's in your Amman office. Is that correct?'

'Hassan Ahmed? Hold the line. I'll put you through.'

No! I wanted to scream. *Stop! I'm not ready!*

My finger twitched automatically to the stop button and cut off the call. It was just as well because Um Khalid's footsteps were on the stairs. She'd come back much sooner than I'd expected. I dropped the phone, flipped back to the emails and pretended to read, my heart beating like a hammer.

'How's it going?' she said, coming over to the desk.

I squeezed my hands together on my lap, trying to stop them trembling and tried to focus my eyes on the screen full of emails.

'It's – it's a bit confusing. I can't quite see . . .'

'Never mind. I'll go through them later. Go and check the store cupboard, *habibti*, and tell me what's running low.'

She went into the beauty room, leaving me shivering at how nearly I'd been caught. I'd need to plan my approach carefully before I tried calling Askil International again.

I mustn't rush, I thought. *One thing at a time.*

CHAPTER THIRTY-THREE

Now that I knew for sure that Uncle Hassan was in Amman, the next step was to find out exactly where he – and Saba – lived, and that meant another phone call. A fresh problem to solve. I couldn't ask Baba or Uncle Yasser or Aunt Zainab to lend me their phone without saying why I wanted it.

My best chance was to call from Perfumes of Paradise, but someone was always coming in and out of the reception area. I'd worked out exactly what I needed to say and practised it again and again. I'd be ready when the chance came.

Malik was out working nearly every day. He'd done such a good job for Uncle Yasser that word had spread. It was illegal for Syrian refugees to work in Jordan, so bosses could pay as little as they liked, but Malik compensated by being brilliant at getting stuff for free.

He came back one day with another solar lamp.

'For your room,' he said, beaming. 'The guy I was working for today said it was broken, but it was easy to fix. You just have to press the switch extra hard.'

The next day I came back from Perfumes of Paradise

and was shocked to find that he'd had taken down the canvas partition to my cubicle.

'Hey! What are you doing?' I burst out angrily.

'What? You don't mind, do you?' he said. 'I thought you'd be pleased. I'm putting in a proper wall. Wooden. You can put hooks on it to hang things from.'

'Oh!'

'I was going to make a bed frame for you too, to lift your mattress off the ground so it doesn't get so damp. But if you'd rather I didn't . . .'

I couldn't get over the feeling of being invaded.

'OK,' I said, 'but . . .'

'But what?'

I pulled myself together.

'But nothing. Thank you. Anything to get rid of that smelly old canvas.'

'I'm not getting rid of it,' he said. 'I'm going to make a little kitchen beside the tent. I'll put in a bench for the cooker, shelves for the plates and pans . . .'

Why was I still feeling annoyed? A kitchen would be great.

He's trying to take over, I told myself. *I thought* I *was the one in charge.*

There was another thing too. If the tent became more like a house, it would mean that we might stay in it forever. I might be trapped here, never living in a house with solid walls again, never going back to school, a refugee for the rest of my life.

He'd turned round to work on the wall.

'There,' he said, standing back to admire his work. 'I'll make your bed frame tomorrow.'

Thanks for the warning, anyway, I thought.

I had to admit, though, that my room was much better. With my lamp I could see what I was doing, and even read in bed, if I could find anything to read.

After supper, I took the dishes outside to wash. The evening was chilly, and squatting over the bucket of cold water was horrible. Malik's plan for a kitchen was great. Why had I been so mean to him?

He came out after me, needing to wash his hands.

'Sorry I wasn't nice about my room,' I said. 'It was – I was surprised, that was all. It's brilliant. Really. And the kitchen's going to be amazing.'

Baba called me from inside the tent.

'Safiya! Where are you?'

'Outside, washing up.'

'Come back in. I want to talk to you.'

What about? I thought anxiously. *Surely he can't have heard about me phoning Askil International?*

I wiped the last plate clean and went inside.

'I've just had a call from my old client,' said Baba, rubbing his hands like he always did when something pleased him. 'He's here! In Jordan!'

My stomach turned over with fright.

'You don't mean that man who came the night we had to run away? The Hawk? But he's . . .'

He frowned.

'Don't call him that, Safiya. It's rude. Abu Mustapha may have a big nose, but . . .'

'Sorry, Baba, but I'm scared of him! It was his fault we had to leave home! What if – if – *they* follow him here? We'd have to run away again!'

Baba patted the mattress beside him.

'Sit down, *ya albi*, my heart. That's not going to happen.'

'But . . .'

He put his arm round me.

'We're safe now. Safe! I feel so bad about you and Tariq, but I had to do what I did. Abu Mustapha is a good man. He needed a lawyer, and I was the only one who would help him. If we don't stand up for justice, what kind of people are we?'

I snuggled against him. This was the old Baba, my real Baba, strong and brave. It felt so lovely sitting there with his arm round me that I stopped listening to what he was saying. I was in my bed at home. I'd had a bad dream and he'd come to me in the night to comfort me and send me back to sleep.

He gave me a nudge.

'Haven't you been listening, little dreamer?'

'Sorry, Baba. What did you say?'

'No salon for you tomorrow. I need you here to get the tent cleaned up, buy some snacks, welcome our guest . . .'

'But Um Khalid . . .'

'She can do without you for once.'

I pulled away from him, annoyed. Why was I always the one who had to give things up?

'There's no point in pretending we're not homeless refugees,' he went on, 'but we can show that we have our self-respect. You need to clean the tent up, Safiya. Put on a good impression. All those dishes over there, and those clothes in a heap . . .'

I flushed. It was true that since I'd been working at Perfumes of Paradise I hadn't kept the tent very well. The floor hadn't been properly swept for days and my kitchen things were piled messily by the entrance flap in a jumble of onions, empty cans, and soot-stained saucepans.

But I'm working now, I thought angrily. *Why can't Tariq help out sometimes? Or Malik? Just because I'm a girl . . .*

'What am I going to tell Um Khalid?' I said unhappily.

Baba pulled out his phone.

'I'll speak to her.'

I made one last try.

'Can't you meet Abu Mustapha in town, Baba? Why does he want to come out here?'

Baba raised his eyebrows.

'Discretion, of course. We don't want the whole world to know our business.'

There was no point in arguing.

CHAPTER THIRTY-FOUR

Once Baba had gone out next morning, I worked like crazy.

'You're not going to look down your beaky nose at us, Mr Snooty,' I muttered as I cleaned up the tent.

I arranged Tariq's schoolbooks where the Hawk would see them as soon as he stepped into the tent.

'See?' I told him. 'We can still read books, you know.'

When it was all done, I ran across to Abu Ali's shop.

He beamed at the sight of me.

'*Alhamdulillah!* I thought you'd given up poor old Abu Ali! I hardly ever see you any more.'

I bought some little cakes, then some shiny red apples and green grapes. They'd look great arranged on a plate.

Back in the tent, I looked around. I was seriously into décor now.

A rug, I thought. *That one Aunt Zainab keeps rolled up under her bed for summer picnics. I've beaten it often enough. Why shouldn't I ask her to lend it to me? She can only say no.*

Before I lost my nerve, I dashed across to the house and knocked on the kitchen door. Aunt Zainab poked her head out of the window.

'What are you doing here? You should be at the salon.'

'I've come to ask you a favour.'

'Now why didn't I guess that?'

'Baba's got a guest coming this afternoon, Aunt. An important man,' I told her proudly.

'Who? What man?'

'An old client from Damascus. Abu Mustapha. The thing is, I need to make a good impression.'

She shut the window.

You old meanie, I thought. *After all I've done to help you.*

But a second later she opened the back door.

'How old are you?' she asked abruptly.

'Thirteen.'

And my birthday was just the other day, I added silently, *if you're thinking of giving me a late birthday present.*

'Hm,' she said. 'Too young to find you a husband. What's this man coming for if it's not for you?'

'*What?*' I almost shouted. She'd driven birthdays right out of my mind. 'Baba wouldn't – he'd never . . .'

She shrugged.

'Don't be so naive. What else is there for you but an early marriage?'

She was making me angry. I had to get her back on track.

'Abu Mustapha's coming on some other business,' I said, talking quickly before my confidence fizzled out. 'I want to make a good impression. Please can I borrow your picnic rug?'

'A good impression?' she scoffed. 'It's a tent, not your posh Damascus apartment!' Then she seemed to pull herself up short and I was surprised to see a flicker of anxiety in her eyes. 'I suppose this grand person will think we're all country bumpkins,' she said uncertainly.

'That's just what I don't want him to think, Aunt,' I said in a softer voice.

'Go on, then,' she said, taking me by surprise. 'Get it. You know where it is. Don't stand there dithering. I'll come over with you.'

I darted to her bedroom and pulled out the picnic rug. Aunt Zainab was in the sitting room when I came out. She piled a couple of embroidered cushions into my arms and picked up two more to carry herself.

'Aunt Zainab!' I gasped. 'This is more than . . .'

'If you think,' she said irritably, 'that I want your guest to look down on us, on *our* family, you don't know me, Safiya. Now, for heaven's sake, let's get on with it.'

An hour later, after Aunt Zainab had finally gone, I stood back to admire the tent.

'If that doesn't impress you, Baba, I'll – I'll run away!' I said out loud.

What a transformation! On the picnic rug, which was a lovely deep crimson colour, I'd set Aunt Zainab's brass tray on its low wooden stand, with her best coffee cups laid out nicely. Cushions from her sitting room were heaped on the mattresses and, most cunning of all, an old striped tablecloth was tacked to the ugly wooden partition.

I've got a talent for this, I thought. *Maybe I could be a set designer on films.*

But there was no time for daydreaming. I needed to tidy myself up before Baba came back. Luckily, Malik had found a broken piece of mirror on a rubbish dump the day before, and had fixed it to the partition. I put on the flowery hijab Um Khalid had given me and fastened it with the pearl pin.

I was only just ready when the gate squeaked open. They were here! Abu Mustapha came in first, but I was watching Baba's eyes open with surprise as he looked round the tent.

I'd only seen the Hawk a couple of times, but I would have recognized that long, lean face, the smooth silver hair and beaky nose anywhere.

I listened carefully as I laid out the cake and made the coffee, but they were only talking about the Azraq roads and the shortage of water. I took the tray over to them, set the fruit bowl beside it and waited.

'Thank you, *habibti*,' said Baba, waving his hand dismissively.

So he wanted me to leave them to it? I wasn't allowed to listen? That meant sitting in my stuffy room with nothing to do.

Then I saw that the Hawk had put a newspaper down on the mattress beside him.

'Excuse me,' I said with a modest smile, 'but may I borrow your newspaper?'

He nodded without looking at me, so I picked the newspaper up and went into my room, trying not to look at Baba, who was frowning at me for pushing myself forward. The paper wouldn't be very interesting but it would be better than staring at the canvas wall for an hour or more.

I sat on my bed, yawning and leafing through it. It was as boring as I'd expected and I was just about to put it down when the words Askil International sprang out at me. Under them was a short announcement: *Askil International has announced that its Middle East headquarters are relocating to Dubai next month.*

My skin prickled with horror. Dubai! I'd never find Saba in Dubai! I had to act quickly, or she'd be lost forever!

CHAPTER THIRTY-FIVE

I leapt to my feet and started pacing the narrow space beside my bed.

I've been wasting time! I thought. *I've just got to find them before they go!*

I sat down on my mattress again.

Maybe I should talk to Baba again. If he knew they were so close and going away so soon, surely he'd be willing to get in touch?

But then I remembered how sad he'd looked when he'd said, *I'd be ashamed for my daughter to see us as we are now.* I didn't want to hurt him again, even though I knew in my heart that he was wrong.

Once I've found Saba she'll show him he was worrying about nothing, I thought. *She'll be thrilled to find us all. I know she will.*

At last the Hawk got up to go and I was able go back into the tent.

'Thank you, sir,' I said, handing him the newspaper.

He hardly glanced at me.

'I'll be in touch next week,' he said to Baba. 'Let me know your bank details so I can transfer the fee for your retainer.'

Baba looked embarrassed.

'I don't actually have an account.'

'Of course.' The Hawk nodded. 'I'll give you cash for now.' He took his wallet out of his pocket and pressed some banknotes into Baba's hand. Then he hesitated. 'It can't be easy living in a place like this,' he said, his face softening. 'I see you've made the best of it. Resourceful. Just like all us Syrians.' He hesitated. 'I know how much you've done for me, Adnan. If you hadn't taken my case and supported me . . .'

Baba interrupted him.

'No, no, you mustn't blame yourself. I've been walking a tightrope for years. I'd had plenty of warnings. Your case just tipped things over the edge.'

'Even so,' the Hawk said, but by then they were out of the tent and walking towards the gate, so I didn't hear the rest.

Baba came back smiling delightedly.

'Well done, Safiya! You worked a miracle!'

'Aunt Zainab lent me the stuff,' I said. 'I've got to take it back.'

'Yes, of course. But we're going to have to keep this standard up. There'll be more visitors from now on, *inshallah*. You're going to be kept busy.'

His praise had made me glow, but now I had a horrible feeling about what he was going to say next.

'You don't need to go to that salon any more,' he went on. 'Abu Mustapha's setting up a business and he wants me to work with him. He was clever enough to get some of his money transferred to an international account before he left Syria. I wish I'd done the same! This is the beginning, Safiya, don't you see?'

I didn't care about Abu Mustapha's business.

'Baba, please! I love going to the salon!' I said desperately. 'I'm learning new stuff all the time. It's like going to school!'

He shook his head.

'No. I need you here. You can go till the end of the week, but then it stops. If I'm going to work with Abu Mustapha, I'll have to entertain clients. The tent needs to be clean and tidy. Proper meals, not just cakes and coffee. Look, you stay here and clear up. I'll take Zainab's things back to her.'

I wanted to pick up the coffee pot and hurl it after him as he grabbed an armful of cushions and went out of the tent.

That's it, then, is it? I shouted in my head. *I'm just a servant! You don't care about me or my future at all!*

I flung myself down on the mattress where the men had been sitting. Something hard was underneath me. I pulled out Baba's mobile phone. It must have fallen out of his pocket.

If I hadn't been so furious with Baba, I don't think I'd have dared to pick it up and switch it on. I scowled into the tiny bright screen, and knew exactly what I had to do next.

'I don't care what you say, Baba,' I said out loud to the empty tent. 'I'm not going to let you keep me and Saba apart any longer.'

I'd learned the Askil number off by heart, but as my fingers hovered over the keyboard, I forced myself to calm down. I couldn't mess things up again.

I punched in the number.

The same girl, with the same bored voice, answered at once.

I put on my grown-up voice and my best Jordanian accent.

'This is Blossoms of Paradise Florist,' I said. 'I have an order for flowers for the family of Hassan Ahmed. Could you kindly give me his home address?'

'Sorry,' the girl at the other end said. 'We don't give out our employees' personal details.'

I was ready for this.

'Oh, I quite understand,' I gushed. 'it's just that I've got a bit of a problem. It's his daughter's birthday soon, and the order's supposed to be a surprise from a family friend in New York.'

I was clutching the phone so tightly that my fingers were starting to cramp. I transferred it to the other hand. The girl was tapping on her keyboard at the other end. She'd stopped listening.

'It's such a shame,' I went on lightly. 'I suppose I'll have to go back to the client and tell her it's not possible.'

The typing stopped.

'Well . . .' the girl said.

'It's a big commission too,' I went on. 'Frankly, it'll be a loss to us if we can't fulfil it. Times are so hard at the moment.'

I held my breath.

'I don't know . . .' the girl began. I could hear the indecision in her voice. 'Look, there's no harm in it, I suppose. All right. Give me a minute. I'll find it for you.'

The seconds ticked by agonizingly slowly. At last she came back.

'I really shouldn't be doing this,' she said doubtfully.

I resisted the urge to plead.

'Well, if it's too much . . . It's a shame for Saba, since it's her birthday. She'd have been so pleased.'

'You know the daughter's name?'

'Of course. It's on the card the client wants us to write.'

'I see. In that case, OK. Here's the address. Have you got a pen?'

My jaw dropped. Why hadn't I thought of that?

'Silly me!' I said breathlessly. 'Hold on a minute.'

I plunged my hand into the pocket of Baba's coat, which he had left lying on the mattress, thanking Allah when my fingers closed round his biro.

'Go ahead.' I wrote the address down on my hand as she read it out. 'Thank you so much! You have no idea what this means . . .'

'What?' She sounded puzzled. I stopped short. I'd

been almost squealing with excitement, and my Jordanian accent had slipped. I was in danger of giving the game away.

'Sorry,' I said, improvising rapidly. 'My colleague's just come in and brought me something. 'Thank you. I really appreciate your help.'

'It's all right,' the girl said. 'But, if anyone asks you, don't tell them it was me who gave it to you.'

'Of course not. Goodbye.'

I put the phone down and punched the air. I'd done it! I'd got Saba's address!

'What do you think of that?' I asked her. 'Clever, or not? Now I've just got to get to Amman and find you.'

But that, I knew, would be much harder.

CHAPTER THIRTY-SIX

As usual, Tariq was late coming back from the bottling plant. I was burning to tell him what I'd discovered, so as I cleared away his dishes I started winking at him and nodding towards the tent entrance.

'What's the matter with you?' he said. 'Got something in your eye?'

'No!' I said. 'I – I just want you to help me take these dishes outside so I can wash up.'

'Do it in the morning,' he yawned.

Then he saw my face, and got it at last.

'Oh, I see. Yes, all right.'

Typical Tariq! No subtlety at all.

Once we were outside, I pulled him away from the tent entrance, out of earshot of Baba and Malik. He listened, goggle-eyed, when I told him what I'd discovered.

'Safiya, you cunning little devil! Blossoms of Paradise! That's brilliant!'

I smirked with pride.

'We've got to get to Amman and find her. Them, I mean. Before they go to Dubai.'

'Yes! Yes, we must! It might be our only chance!' He

frowned. 'But how? I mean, Amman's miles away and we don't know our way around. Think of the cost! Buses, taxis . . .'

He was right, of course. I hadn't thought it all through.

'Um Khalid might lend me a bit,' I said doubtfully.

'Safiya, you know that's ridiculous. Why should she? And, anyway, you can't ask her. No, the only thing to do is to tell Baba.'

'Yes, but you know what he'll say, that Saba will be upset, he promised Uncle Hassan, he's ashamed of being a poor refugee, blah blah.'

'Blah blah or not, they're good reasons. And I don't want to go behind his back. He'd be furious if we did. And, what's worse, he'd be upset and disappointed in us. Look, why don't I speak to Baba? Maybe I could talk him round. It's just so . . . so incredible to think of our own sister, a few miles away, and we can't even . . . I'll talk to him now if you like.'

He turned to go back into the tent. I caught his sleeve.

'No! He'll only put you off again. Give it a few more days. I've got a feeling in my bones that something's going to turn up.'

'Well, all right. But don't leave it too long.' Then he smiled. 'Isn't it great about Abu Mustapha giving Baba work? Maybe things really will change and he'll make Baba a partner and we can move somewhere decent. He wouldn't be ashamed any more. We'd be able to hold our heads up again. It'll be much better if he contacts Uncle

Hassan himself, don't you see?'

He was right, but his reasonableness infuriated me. I gave the bucket a kick. It clanged loudly.

Baba appeared at the tent entrance.

'What are you two doing out there? Come back inside. It's time we all went to bed.'

CHAPTER THIRTY-SEVEN

The weather was getting worse. Sometimes ice crunched underfoot in the mornings and Malik had to keep deepening the trench to stop the tent from flooding every time there was a rainstorm. We couldn't keep the cold out, and our blankets were too thin to warm us properly at night. After supper I'd light the gas stove and we'd huddle round it, stretching out our hands towards the ring of little blue flames, trying to warm up before we went to bed. Being warm had been one of the lovely things at Perfumes of Paradise. I was going to miss it badly.

'Oh, *habibti*, here you are!' said Um Khalid, as I pushed open the salon door on my last day. 'Such a pity you can't stay on. I didn't know how much I needed help till you started here.'

I hardly heard her. I couldn't take my eyes off the girl who was sitting in my place behind the reception desk.

'Jamila's taking over from you,' Um Khalid rattled on. My eyes opened wide in disbelief. 'You can show her what to do. I'll leave you girls to it. My first client's waiting already.'

'*Sabah alkheer*,' Jamila said smugly. 'You're Syrian, aren't you?'

The word *refugee* hovered unspoken in the air.

'From Damascus,' I said as lightly as I could. 'The gleaming pearl of the east. Once.' I took off my stained old jacket and hung it on the hook behind the door. 'I hope you're good at maths. The accounts need keeping up to date all the time.'

Got you, I thought as she blinked uncertainly.

'Um Khalid didn't say anything about that. I'm sure she doesn't expect me to—'

'And then you have to keep the storeroom clean and tidy, check when things are running out and order more, answer the phone, book in appointments, deal with queries from suppliers . . .'

'But I thought . . .'

'You thought what?'

'I thought I'd be doing beauty treatments. Facials and things like that.'

'Really?' I was enjoying myself now. 'You have to have a qualification before you can do all that stuff. Get on a course. Pass exams. There's loads of science in it. Chemistry.'

She was looking like a frightened rabbit.

'Didn't she explain? How did you get this job, anyway?'

'Mama thought – I wasn't much good at school to be honest, and I've always liked make-up and stuff. Um Khalid's my mama's cousin.'

I took pity on her. I'd lost the job, anyway. Being mean to Jamila wouldn't bring it back. Besides, she was the first girl of my age I'd talked to since we'd left home all those months ago.

'Why don't I show you what to do?' I said. 'See how you get on?'

It was slow work teaching Jamila. I did my best, but she had to have everything explained at least twice, and the paperwork put her into a tailspin of panic. At the end of the afternoon we still had our heads bent over it when I looked up to see that Um Khalid was watching us.

'Your mother's downstairs, Jamila,' she said. 'She's come to pick you up.'

Jamila leaped to her feet as if she'd been released from torture, grabbed her coat and made for the door.

'Good luck!' I called after her. She turned her head and gave me a wan smile.

'She'll get the hang of it,' I said patronizingly. 'But I think the accounts might be beyond her.'

Um Khalid was frowning towards the door through which Jamila had disappeared. I had a flash of inspiration.

'I'm sure Baba would let me come back sometimes to help,' I said, as casually as I could.

'Oh, do you think so?' She gave me a quick hug, taking me by surprise. Then she stood back and held me by the arms. 'You're wonderful, Safiya. I hope you know that. I really admire you.'

I wasn't used to praise. It made me want to cry.

'Here.' She reached under the reception desk and pulled out a carrier bag. 'It's a little leaving present. Go on. Take a look.'

My hand was already in the bag. I pulled out a soft blue woollen jacket, thigh-length and warm, with a thick, fake-fur collar.

'It's beautiful!' I gasped.

'Not exactly new, I'm afraid. It was my sister's. She's got too fat for it. It'll keep you warm, anyway.'

'I – I love it!' I could hardly get the words out.

A car horn sounded outside.

'There's Abu Tewfik. Go on. Oh, and . . .' She slid an envelope into my hand. 'Open it when you get home.'

My throat had tightened up.

'Um Khalid, you've been lovely. I can't tell you how much—'

'No, no, *habibti*. No tears. Look, this isn't goodbye, after all. Those accounts! You're right. Jamila's as hopeless as I am. I'll still need you sometimes. One day a week, perhaps.'

I climbed into the taxi behind Abu Tewfik, who was groaning away behind the steering wheel, and tore open the envelope. 10JD! Riches!

I knew at once what I'd get. My feet had been growing and the shoes I'd bought in another life, that day with Farah, had started pinching painfully. It was time to get a pair that would fit from one of the second-hand shoe stalls I'd passed on the way to Perfumes of Paradise.

CHAPTER THIRTY-EIGHT

'Your Baba came by earlier,' said Abu Ali when I slipped across to the shop to buy food for supper. 'He says you won't be needing the charity food box any more.'

'B-but . . .' I stammered.

Then I saw that he was smiling.

'Don't worry. I told him you have to give three months' notice. It makes things complicated if you suddenly withdraw.'

'You made that up, didn't you?' I said.

He pretended to be insulted.

'Who? Me? Never told a lie in my life. But that Baba of yours, he's not the one who has to do the shopping and worry about buying enough food for you all, is he?'

For the second time that day, someone's kindness was making me want to cry.

'Abu Ali, you are, you are . . .' I couldn't get the words out.

He was scratching the top of his bald head, pretending he'd just remembered something.

'And, while I think of it, the charity left these for you to pick up.' He pulled a couple of enormous zip-up bags from under the counter. 'One-off extras for people in tents. Winter supplies. Don't pretend you're warm enough at night! Four blankets. I didn't like to give them to your father. I thought he might . . .'

Refuse to take them, I finished for him in my head. *Don't worry! I won't let him!*

'You'll talk him round.' He was beaming at me. 'Now then, what did you come in for this afternoon?'

'What's in those bags?' asked Baba as I shuffled off my shoes at the entrance to the tent, and put down my bulky load.

'Blankets.' I was watching him anxiously. 'From the charity. It's part of what they do. They left them for us with Abu Ali.'

'That old rascal! He spun me a story about not being able to stop the food boxes. Nonsense, of course, but I didn't want to seem ungrateful. You'll have to take them back, say something polite, tell him . . .'

'Yes, Baba,' I said meekly. 'If you like. But I'm really cold at night. Sometimes I can't go to sleep and I'm starting to get chilblains on my hands. Look. And it's only the beginning of December.'

He sighed impatiently.

'Oh, all right. When I'm back on my feet, I'll make a donation to cover all this. Now, Safiya, Abu Mustapha has just called me. He's coming again on Monday. We'll need . . .'

But I'd stopped listening. I'd unzipped one of the bags and was fingering the thick purple blanket. I could hardly wait to snuggle under it when I got into bed.

'. . . so we'll go into town tomorrow to get a few things for the tent. A rug and so on,' Baba finished. 'Were you listening to me, Safiya?'

Malik had come in. He was standing behind Baba, signalling to me with his eyes. I tried to concentrate on what Baba was saying.

'You want to go shopping?' I said, watching Malik who was shaking his head and pointing to himself, then to me, then back to himself again.

Unlike my dear brother Tariq, I'm great at picking up signals, I gave Malik a tiny nod.

'Haven't you got enough to worry about, Baba?' I said. 'Why don't you let me go with Uncle Malik?'

Baba's phone rang again.

'All right. I'll leave it to you.' He picked up the phone and waved us away. 'Abu Sami! *Kifek?* How are you? I was just going to ring you and . . .'

'That was a good idea,' I whispered to Malik. 'Baba's hopeless at shopping. He'd have spent all his money at once.'

Malik nodded.

'Takes practice to sniff out a bargain. We'll go on Saturday. I'll ask around at Friday prayers and get an idea of what's available.'

'You're going to prayers at the mosque?'

I don't know why I was surprised. Unlike Baba and Tariq, Malik prayed regularly in the tent, carefully making sure that he faced Mecca, while I had let the habit slip.

My question seemed to surprise him too.

'Why do you ask?' he asked.

'I don't know. We're not really religious, I suppose.'

'Faith keeps me going,' he said simply. 'There've been times when it was all I had.'

CHAPTER THIRTY-NINE

Shopping with Malik was the best fun. He'd only been in Azraq a couple of months, but he'd sussed out every shop and business in town while he was looking for work.

'I hope Adnan's not expecting miracles,' he said as we walked into town. 'Azraq's hardly a beacon of style.'

Just for a moment, he'd sounded like Auntie Shirin when she was being sarcastic. He was more like his big sister than he knew. I felt a sudden pang. I hadn't realized how much I'd missed my starchy old aunt.

I soon began to notice that while we were shopping Malik was doing a little business of his own.

'That downpipe's loose,' he'd say to a shopkeeper as we picked through a pile of gaudy cushion covers. 'Needs fixing before the next rainstorm. I could do it tomorrow if you like. Now about those rugs over there . . .'

'Uncle Malik, you're awesome,' I said as we walked home, rugs hanging over his shoulders and both our arms weighted down with bags. 'You've got jobs lined up all next week, and we hardly spent anything! Baba will be stunned!'

'He won't notice,' Malik said. 'When it comes to

practical stuff, my dear brother's no more use than a baby.'

There was Auntie Shirin's voice again. I looked sideways at him. He'd put on weight, muscle rather than fat, and walked confidently. I couldn't see in him the starving, desperate boy who'd been so scared of his big brother.

He was right about Baba. He took our success for granted.

'Very good,' he said, glancing over the treasures we displayed to him. 'I'll be back later. I'm going over to see Yasser.'

I couldn't wait to get started on arranging everything and I'd expected Malik to help, but he went back outside.

'Where are you going?' I called after him.

'To start on your kitchen,' he called back.

Snowball ran into the tent and began to coil her tail round my legs.

'There you are!' I said happily, bending down to scratch between her ears. 'I haven't seen you for days. Now don't get in my way. I've got a lot to do.'

It took me all afternoon to arrange the tent while Malik hammered and sawed outside. Tariq, who'd been working at the bottling station all day, came in just as I finished. He stood at the tent entrance, taking in through narrowed eyes the two rugs, the bright cushions sitting on our new pink and purple blankets, the low coffee table with the wonky leg which Malik was going to fix, the chrome tray, sparkling glasses and colourful bowls for snacks, and the lamp, my favourite thing of all, made of perforated metal in a traditional style, through which a candle would glow prettily.

'Where did all this come from? Safiya, you haven't been . . .'

I rolled my eyes.

'Honestly, Tariq. You're obsessed. Since you ask, it's all bought and paid for. In a roundabout sort of way. Ask Malik.'

He glared at me.

'*Paid* for? What with? I can see I've been wasting my time.'

'What do you mean?'

'Slogging my guts out heaving water bottles around for a few miserable JD while you had a fortune stashed away to spend on all this stuff.'

'Tariq! That's not fair! Malik's paying for most of it by doing jobs for the shopkeepers. We only spent a bit of the money Baba got from his new client.'

'Oh yes? And what's *a bit of money*?'

I told him how much we'd spent.

'Stop trying it on, Safiya. This lot must have cost ten times that.'

I bent down to pick up a corner of the nearest rug.

'There's a tear in it, see? We didn't have to give a cent for it! Malik's going to mend the guy's gutter. That cloth, the one I've pinned over the shuttering, it's got a huge stain in the corner you can't even see. He threw that in as well.'

'Well, if you say so.'

He didn't look convinced.

'Anyway, doing all this, it's a – sort of like an investment. In case Abu Mustapha brings any business people with him.'

'Yes. I suppose . . .'

'You know what Baba's like with money, Tariq. He hasn't got a clue. We're going to need your earnings as much as ever if we want to eat, especially now that I can't work at the salon any more. But I'll manage on as little as I can, so you can keep something for yourself. You need warmer clothes for a start.'

He screwed up his nose, looking sheepish, then pulled open his jacket to show me the thick sweater he was wearing underneath it.

'Where did you get that from? It looks almost new.'

'Aunt Zainab gave it to me. It belonged to Fares but he's too big for it now.'

I burst out laughing.

'You cheat! Who's taking charity now?'

'OK, but it's not exactly charity. I told you. It doesn't fit Fares any more.'

'Lucky you,' I said. 'Aunt Zainab's got a soft spot for you in that stony old heart of hers.'

'Oh,' he said, yawning. 'She's not so bad when you get to know her.'

I scowled at him.

'You don't know the half of it.'

He was reaching for his books already.

'Get me some tea would you, Safiya?' he said. 'I'm struggling to keep awake and I've got a mountain of homework to do.'

I went outside to boil up some water and stopped short in amazement. I'd thought Malik was making a sort of canvas cubbyhole, but he'd built a proper room, with chipboard walls like the one in my bedroom, and even a real floor, made of strips of wood raised above the muddy ground.

'It's – wow! It's huge!' was all I could say.

'I'll take down this bit of tent wall when it's finished,' he said, standing aside to let me look in. 'You'll be able to hook it back to get in and out from inside the tent. Let me get on, will you? I've got to fix the tarpaulin over the roof in case it rains tonight.'

I stepped out of his way.

'Uncle Malik, it's incredible! Where did you get the wood and poles and all that?'

'Didn't you notice them?' He was talking through a screw clamped between his lips. 'I've been stockpiling things behind the tent. I'll do the bench and shelves tomorrow. Now if you don't mind . . .'

I went back into the tent.

'He's amazing, isn't he?' said Tariq. 'This place is getting to be more like home.'

I shuddered.

'It'll never be like home. Have you forgotten what a home is? It's a house with walls. Solid walls. This is a cold, smelly old tent. It always will be, and I can't wait to get out of it.'

But later, as I dished up the supper I'd made — chickpea stew with a few pieces of lamb for flavour and large helpings of fluffy rice — I looked around the tent. In the soft light of the solar lamp it looked almost nice, I had to admit. I'd never get used to the mud and dirt, the chemical toilet, the bucket of cold water to wash in, the cold and the damp. I'd never stop missing our proper bathroom, the hot shower, the TV, electricity, Farah . . .

I stopped myself before I got upset.

Take a look round, Saba, I told my twin. *We've made something of this, haven't we? We don't need to feel ashamed, whatever Baba says.*

CHAPTER FORTY

Aunt Zainab came rattling in through the gate soon after breakfast the next day.

'So this is what all the banging and sawing was about,' she said, pursing her lips at the unfinished extension.

'Uncle Malik's making me a kitchen,' I said, watching her face uneasily.

'I hope he asked Yasser's permission. This isn't your land, you know. We'd be within our rights to charge you rent.'

My mouth fell open. I couldn't think of anything to say, so I shut it again.

Aunt Zainab was walking round the outside of the new kitchen, testing the strength of the struts, tapping the chipboard wall and peering inside to check the wooden floor.

'He's got money, then, to pay for all this,' she said at last.

'He didn't have to buy any of it!' I wasn't sure if she'd approve or not. 'It's all off-cuts from where he's been working. Rejects, look, like this piece of wood that's split up the middle. He's managed to use it, anyway. He's brilliant at getting stuff cheaply, Aunt. Come and see what we got on Saturday.'

I led her into the tent, half wanting to show it off to her, half dreading her reaction.

She was impressed, I could tell, though she certainly wasn't going to say so.

'Baba's old client's coming again. We can't keep on borrowing things from you. Would you like some tea, Aunt?'

She waved the offer aside.

'What on earth did all this cost?'

I couldn't wait to tell her.

'Well,' she said at last, after poking her nose into everything. 'Let's hope the investment pays off.' She took a final look round, and I knew she was trying to find something to criticize.

'That kettle's got soot marks up the side,' she said with satisfaction. 'You'd better clean it up before all your grand visitors come calling and think they can look down on us.'

I followed her to the entrance to the tent. It had been a dull, cloudy day, but the sun had suddenly come out. She looked back at me as she shuffled around with her feet to put her shoes on.

'What's that on your face?' she said.

I put my hand up to touch my cheek.

'I don't know. It's itchy.'

'You get a lot of nasty rashes here in the winter. The desert dust is full of germs when it's wet. It's not like Damascus here, you know. I suppose I'll have to give you a cream for it. Don't scratch it or it'll get infected. Scarred for life, probably. Then you'll be sorry.'

By Sunday morning, the rash had spread all the way down my left cheek. It itched all the time and the cream Aunt Zainab had given me hadn't helped at all.

She called me over after breakfast to help her shake out her rugs. I was glad to see that Um Salim was there, perched on a chair by the table.

'You've been scratching that thing on your face,' Aunt Zainab said accusingly as I came in through the back door. 'I warned you, Safiya.'

'I haven't!' I said indignantly.

It wasn't quite true. The itch screamed to be scratched, and sometimes I hadn't been able to resist.

Um Salim leaned forward to get a better look.

'You poor thing,' she said. 'Haven't you got any cream for it?'

'I gave her some,' said Aunt Zainab. 'She's been scratching.'

'It looks infected. She needs to see a skin specialist,' said Um Salim.

'How's she going to afford a skin specialist?' scoffed Aunt Zainab. 'She just needs to stop picking at it.'

I wasn't going to put up with her any longer. I made the first excuse I could think of that would get me out of the house.

'I'm sorry, Aunt Zainab, but I came to say that I can't help you today,' I said. 'Baba's client's coming this afternoon.'

Aunt Zainab frowned. Um Salim smiled.

'That's good,' she said. 'Off you go, dear, and look after that face of yours.'

I felt a bit worried having told the lie, because Aunt Zainab would be bound to notice if nobody came, but when I got back to the tent Baba was putting his phone back in his pocket.

'Abu Mustapha's coming this afternoon instead of tomorrow, Safiya.' He had his business face on again. 'Make sure everything's ready.'

Alhamdulillah, I breathed.

Allah was looking out for me, after all.

CHAPTER FORTY-ONE

Now here's a bit of wisdom from me, Safiya Adnan, aged thirteen.

In this life you never know what's going to happen.

I mean, think about it. How could I have known I'd have to bolt out of my nice ordinary life in Damascus like a rabbit out of its burrow? Or that Malik would turn up out of the blue to make our lives easier? Or that I'd get a job in a beauty salon?

And I could never, ever have foreseen what was going to happen next.

The Hawk's visit was the same as the first time. I served coffee and snacks and went into my nice new kitchen to do some cooking, then came out to say goodbye when he was about to leave.

As usual, his eyes swept past me, then they swooped back again.

'That's a nasty rash,' he said to Baba. 'You should get a doctor to look at it. Bring her to Amman with you tomorrow. My cousin Hannan's a skin specialist. She won't charge.'

I honestly thought I'd pass out. Amman! I was going to Amman!

And then I wanted to scream with frustration because Baba said, 'That's very kind, but, honestly, there's no need. We can't possibly trouble Dr Hannan. I'm sure she's much too busy.'

I was just plucking up my courage to say, 'But it hurts, Baba, dreadfully, and Aunt Zainab said I might be scarred for life,' when the Hawk (only now I knew that he was really an angel sent from Heaven) said, 'Nonsense. I'll call you this evening to give you directions and tell you what time Hannan can see you.'

Then Baba walked with him to the gate, and they stopped for a final chat.

I couldn't stop myself from jumping up and down.

Saba! Did you hear that? I told my twin. *Get ready, girl. I'm coming to Amman! Look out for me. Show yourself somehow, please. We've got to meet tomorrow — this might be our only chance!*

Then the hinges squeaked as Baba shut the gate.

He looked worried when he came back into the tent.

'My poor girl!' he said, holding my chin in his hand and looking closely at the rash. 'How could I have let it go this far? I thought your aunt was treating you.'

'Her cream didn't work, Baba. It really does hurt now. I think the – I mean Abu Mustapha – was right. It is infected.'

'Well, don't worry. His cousin will put it right for you.' He pinched my chin gently before he let it go. 'A trip to Amman, eh? A real outing for you. We'll have to get up early to make sure of catching the bus.'

CHAPTER FORTY-TWO

'What time does the bus go?' I asked Baba as we hurried along the road into town early the following day. The sun hadn't even come up and I was half dazzled by the headlights of cars and trucks coming towards us.

'No exact time. It leaves when it's full of passengers. And there's only one bus a day so keep up, Safiya. We've left it a bit late as it is.'

I was already walking as fast as I could but now I broke into a trot. I'd have sprinted if Baba had let me, even though my feet were killing me. They'd grown a lot in the last couple of weeks and I had to walk with my toes curled up inside my shoes.

We could hear the roar of the bus's heavy diesel engine as we hurried into the bus station. It was nearly full and people were pushing to get on. We just made it on board before the door was slammed shut.

There were only single seats left, but a young man noticed us and politely moved so that Baba and I could be together. I was really grateful because it meant I could sit by the window.

The countryside around Azraq had been brown and

bare all summer, but now some scraggy sheep were grazing on patches that the rain had turned green. The refugee camp in the distance looked like a settlement on an alien planet, straight out of a sci-fi movie.

Everything looked depressing.

Baba was right, I thought. *Saba wouldn't like Azraq at all. I'd hate her to come here. Meeting us would only upset her.*

'You've gone pale, *habibti*,' Baba said suddenly. 'You're not going to be sick, are you?'

I tried to smile.

'No, I'm fine, Baba. Really.'

I'd talked myself into a better place by the time we hit the honking, crawling traffic outside Amman.

I've got to trust her! I told myself. *She's just like me and I'd be amazed and excited if I didn't know I had a twin, and then found out that I did. Of course she'll want to know me!*

The bus was crawling along a valley. Square, cream-coloured houses were stacked like boxes up the steep hillsides. Would one of those be Saba's house? Did she run down one of those long flights of stairs between the buildings every day on her way to school?

Maybe Uncle Hassan's place is like that one, I thought as we passed a pale stone house with a pretty iron balcony, arched windows and pencil-thin dark green cypress trees sprouting up beside it like exclamation marks.

I was starting to feel small and silly. How could I possibly have imagined that in this big, crowded city I could find one girl? I'd stupidly imagined that we'd simply bump into each other, that I'd spot her in a crowd, or that she'd see me and . . . Now that I was here, looking down on the mass of cars and people in the maze of streets, that stupid dream faded to nothing.

We chugged off the road at last into the bus station. Everyone was pushing to get off, but I held back. I was so down-hearted I felt like staying on the bus and going straight back to Azraq.

Baba was frowning at me.

'Have you got a fever? A headache?'

I made myself get up out of my seat.

'Sorry, Baba. I'm coming.'

I was dazed as we walked out through the bus station, and Baba had to grab my hand to pull me out of the way of a bus lumbering out of its stand.

'Come on!' he shouted above the roar of its engine. 'The clinic's not far. We'll walk.'

I groaned inside. My toes felt raw. I was sure there were blisters all over them.

It was quite a climb out of the valley up to the quieter streets above. There were nice apartment buildings here, three or four storeys high, with plants in front of them and big balconies.

Amman's not bad, I thought. *Not as good as Damascus, of course. It's a million times nicer than Azraq, anyway.*

Baba was looking at the names of the buildings as we went past.

'Here it is!' he said at last, walking up the steps to the entrance.

The clinic had polished wooden floors and a clean doctor-ish smell, just like our old doctor's office at home. Dr Hannan was waiting for us. She looked too young and pretty to be a consultant doctor. She had dangly earrings and she wasn't wearing a hijab.

'This kind of winter rash is very common in the desert areas,' she said. 'I'll give you an ointment to clear it up. It'll help with the spots too.'

'Will I — will there be a scar?' I dared to ask.

She laughed.

'No! Your face will be as good as new.'

I melted inside with relief. I'd been trying not to think about how awful I might look.

A few minutes later, I was following Baba back down the steps to the street.

'It's too far to walk to Abu Mustapha's place,' he said. 'We'll have to get a taxi.'

I smiled at him gratefully. My feet were agony now. I hobbled down the hill after him to the crossroads, where heavy traffic was moving down the main road. Baba hurried on ahead of me so fast that I couldn't keep up with him.

He reached the corner and raised his arm to hail a taxi, then stepped off the pavement to make sure the driver saw him. And then, out of nowhere, another car zoomed recklessly past the taxi on the inside.

'Baba!' I screamed. 'Watch out!'

It was too late. There was a hideous squeal of brakes and a deafening crash of metal on metal. And then a horrible, horrible silence.

For what seemed like an age I stood frozen to the spot. Ahead of me, the people who had been waiting to cross the road were crowding round the accident. I couldn't see Baba at all. I dashed forward, clawing them out of the way.

Baba was lying on the ground, his eyes closed, and blood from his head was pooling on to the tarmac.

'Baba!' I heard myself yelling. 'Open your eyes! Look at me! You're not dead. You can't be! Someone help him! Please!'

I threw myself down on the ground beside him. His eyes were closed and his face was a pale sickly colour. People were shouting and jostling all round me.

Someone took my elbow, forcing me to stand up.

'Let me look,' a man said. 'I know first aid.'

He leaned over Baba and checked his pulse.

'Good and strong,' he said.

'He's not dead? Oh! Oh!' I sank down beside him again.

'I've called an ambulance!' someone else called out. 'It's on the way.'

A woman put her arm round me and lifted me up again.

'Don't cry, *habibti*! Didn't you hear the man say? He's

alive! They're going to get him to the hospital. He'll be fine.'

A furious argument was going on behind her. The taxi driver and the man who had crashed into him were yelling at each other.

'Where do you live, dear?' the woman was asking me.

'I – I'm from Azraq,' I stammered. 'We only came for the day. Baba's got a meeting. We were going there now.'

I was shivering uncontrollably.

Sirens sounded and suddenly two policemen appeared.

'Tell them Baba's name, *habibti,*' the woman said.

An ambulance had arrived now. The ambulance men had opened the back and pulled out a stretcher. I struggled out of the woman's grasp.

'What are you doing? Where are you taking him? Is he going to be all right?'

'Your Baba, is he?' one of the men said. 'Got a nasty bang on the head, hasn't he? Can't tell you any more till we get him to the hospital. He'll be fine, *inshallah.*'

'Don't shut the door! Take me with you!' I was frantically trying to climb in after Baba. 'Don't leave me here!'

'Can't do that, *habibti*, sorry,' the other man said. 'You go home. Call the hospital later.' He turned to the other man. 'Did you get his name?'

'Where are you taking him?' I screamed.

'The Al Bashir,' he called back, then he climbed in after the stretcher and pulled the door shut. A minute later the ambulance was driving away, its blue light flashing and the siren wailing.

CHAPTER FORTY-THREE

I stood still, too shocked to move. This was how Mama had died. Surely Allah would not take Baba in this way too?

The kind woman was shaking my arm again.

'Haven't you got any relatives in Amman?'

'No! I . . .'

The taxi driver and the other man were still hurling accusations at each other while a policeman tried to question them.

'You don't know anyone here? No one at all?'

'Just – I've got an uncle, but I . . .'

'An uncle!' She smiled with relief. 'That's good. Where does he live?'

'In Um Uthania.'

'That's not too far from here. Look, let me call my daughter. I was going to meet her, but there's no hurry. We'll get a taxi and I'll take you to your uncle's place. You know the street and the number?'

'Yes, but I'm not supposed to . . .'

'Um Uthania's a nice district.'

She was looking at me doubtfully. I saw myself through

her eyes: my blue coat – which had seemed smart in Azraq but which looked old-fashioned in Amman – my cracked shoes and the awful rash on my face. I felt my insides begin to melt in panic, and took a deep, shuddering breath to control it.

'Your real uncle, is he? Jordanian?' she went on. 'Only you've got a Syrian accent. I hope you don't mind me asking.'

'My mother was Jordanian. He's her brother. But I don't think I should . . .'

'He's your family, my lovely, that's all that matters.' She was sounding brisk now. I'd become a problem that she was keen to solve.

She was still holding my arm, walking me along the street away from the crash site. Before I knew what was happening, she had lifted her arm and a taxi drew up by the kerb.

'I've only got a few JD on me,' I said. 'I can't . . .'

'That's all right.' She was pushing me ahead of her into the back of the taxi. 'It's nothing. I can't leave you here in the middle of Amman, a young girl like you.' She leaned forward. 'Um Uthania,' she said to the taxi driver.

My stomach was churning in panic. I kept seeing Baba's still, white face as he lay on the pavement, blood trickling from the side of his head. What if those people had been lying to me? What if he was really badly hurt? How could I be going off like this, when I ought to be at the hospital with him? And how could I turn up, out of the blue, at Uncle Hassan's house where Saba would be? It was all crazy, wrong, upside down. It was like living through a terrible dream.

By the time the taxi had pulled up outside a small apartment block in a quiet back street, my brain had started working again. Baba was the only thing that mattered now. Getting help for him was what I had to do.

The woman had been looking at her watch.

'Do you want me to come in with you? Only . . .'

'No, thank you,' I said quickly. I would much rather tackle this alone. I gave her a shaky smile. *'Alf shukr!* Thank you so much! I don't know what I'd have done without you.'

'It's nothing. It's all the will of Allah. Look, don't worry. Everything will be all right, I'm sure.'

Her phone rang. She fished it out of her bag as I got out of the taxi.

'No, no, Zahra, don't worry. I'm coming now. Everything's fine. I just had to . . .'

I shut the taxi door and watched it drive away, then stood still for a moment, summoning my courage. I'd never felt so alone in my whole life. But right then, just when I needed it, the voice of my mother was there in my head.

Go on, Safiya. Go on.

So I put back my shoulders and marched up the short flight of steps to the building's entrance.

There was an entry phone by the door. I stood there

with my finger hovering over the number of Uncle Hassan's flat. How could I explain, into a crackly answerphone, who I was and why I'd come?

Anyway, Uncle Hassan must be at work and Saba will be at school, I thought. *There'll be no one at home.*

I was still dithering when someone clattered down the staircase inside the building and pushed open the frosted glass door. It was a young man in paint-splashed clothes.

'You want to come in?' he said, holding the door open for me. 'Mind the wall. The paint's wet.'

I nodded and stepped inside. Nothing seemed real any more.

There were two doors on each landing. On the first floor, the door on the right had a brass plate with Uncle Hassan's name on it. I said a prayer, and pressed the bell.

The wait was agonizing. A minute passed. It felt like an hour. At last, when I'd almost given up hope, the door opened so suddenly that I jumped back. A small round woman with streaks of grey in her thick black hair was standing on the doormat, staring at me, her eyes widening with horror as she took in the sight of me.

'Aunt Israa?' I said. 'It's – it's Safiya. Is Uncle Hassan here? I have to—'

'No!' she shouted. 'I don't know you! This is a trick! Go away!'

She slammed the door in my face. I reeled back as if she'd actually punched me. This was worse, much worse, than I'd expected.

What could I do? Who could help me? If only I could find the Hawk! But I didn't even know his full name, and Baba had never told me where he worked.

Now all I wanted was to get away. I'd only seen Aunt Israa for a few seconds, but she'd looked at me as if I was a snake about to strike. I couldn't face seeing her again.

I was just about to go back down the stairs, when I heard the front door open below. A man's deep voice said, 'Good, they've started decorating at last. Watch out. The paint's wet.'

Two pairs of footsteps were on the stairs. The man rounded the last corner and came into view. He was quite short, grey haired, with deep-set eyes.

He stopped dead when he saw me.

'What's the matter, Baba? Who is it?' said a girl's voice.

She stepped out from behind him, and there she was, my double, my sister, my Saba, my twin.

CHAPTER FORTY-FOUR

I'd imagined this moment a million times, but it was all going wrong. Saba didn't even recognize me. She just looked puzzled and scornful. There wasn't time for more. The door of the flat shot open and Aunt Israa darted out, flapping her arms like a demented chicken.

'Saba! Come inside! At once!'

She grabbed Saba's arm and dragged her towards the door.

'What's going on?' Saba said. 'Who's that girl? Stop pulling me, Mama. I'm coming.'

She spoke Arabic with a Jordanian accent but her voice was high and light like mine and the braces on her teeth gave her a kind of lisp.

I heard Aunt Israa say, 'It's no one, darling. A Syrian beggar. How was school? Did the test go all right?'

Just before the door slammed shut, Saba turned to look at me again. She said, 'That's so weird. That girl looks exactly like . . .' Then she and Aunt Israa had gone and Uncle Hassan and I were standing on the landing, staring at each other.

'Uncle Hassan . . .' I began.

He looked shaken, as if he didn't know what to do.

'Yes, I'm your uncle Hassan,' he said at last. 'And you're Safiya. I recognized you at once. Whatever are you doing in Jordan? How on earth did you find us? Where's your father?'

'That's why I've come!' I said. 'Baba was hit by a car! He's been taken to hospital! He . . .'

My legs gave way and I staggered. Uncle Hassan took hold of my arm and steadied me.

'What did you say? An accident? Which hospital? Where?'

'The Al Bashir, I think the ambulance man said.'

He led me towards the stairs.

'We'll go there right now. Don't cry, Safiya. Tell me all about it on the way.'

A few minutes later, we were driving fast along a big motorway, and words were tumbling out of me. I told Uncle Hassan how we'd escaped from Damascus and gone to live with Uncle Yasser, how Baba had met the Hawk again, and how the accident had happened. I talked so fast I wasn't sure if he'd understood anything at all.

I ran out of words at last. Uncle Hassan didn't say anything, and I started to feel worried.

'I'm really sorry, Uncle Hassan!' I said at last as we turned into a quieter road. 'I know I shouldn't have come. Baba told me that Saba doesn't know about me – about us – but I didn't know what else to do.'

He turned and gave me a quick, reassuring smile.

'You did the right thing and I'm very pleased to meet you at last, Safiya. I'd heard on the grapevine that Adnan was in trouble and had been trying to get out of Syria. I've been trying to contact him through friends, in fact, but you know how careful we all have to be. I didn't want to make things worse for him. I had no idea you were in Jordan! If I'd known, of course, we'd have . . .' He paused, as if he was trying to find the right words. 'It can't be easy for you to understand why we – your aunt in particular – felt that Saba shouldn't know . . .'

I rushed in to help him out.

'Baba explained,' I said. 'I mean, about how she's sensitive and everything and how you'd agreed not tell her about us. About me. I do understand, really I do. I've only just found out myself that our mother was ill after we were born. I've always known I had a twin, though. I've been so – well – lonely, I suppose. I thought we could be such close . . .' I had to stop to control my voice. 'I've longed to meet her, especially since we had to leave home, but Baba made me see – I mean, I couldn't bear it if she met us and was ashamed of us.'

'Ashamed? No!' Uncle Hassan's hands were gripping the steering wheel so strongly that his knuckles were white. 'None of us could possibly be ashamed of you! How could we be when nothing that's happened is your fault?' He braked sharply as a rickety van with an open back, piled high with mattresses, swerved in front of him.

'You want to kill us all?' he shouted through the

windscreen. 'Go ahead! Be my guest!'

'Baba says we should wait till we're back on our feet,' I went on. 'I mean at the moment, we're just refugees, living in a tent, and . . .'

I stopped. I hadn't meant to give so much away.

'You're living in a tent?' He sounded appalled. 'But at least you're going to school?'

'No. The school in Azraq was full. Anyway, Baba needs me to do the cooking and washing and stuff.'

His face had darkened.

I'm making everything worse! He thinks I'm begging! I thought.

Aloud I said, 'It's all right, Uncle. We're fine, really. Tariq's going to school. He's got a job in a bottling plant too. Afternoons and weekends. He earns 3JD a day and gives all of it to me for the food and everything. And my uncle Malik – he's Baba's half-brother – he's living with us now and he's really helpful. He gets building jobs sometimes and gives me some money. And now that Baba's working with Abu Mustapha, perhaps . . .'

I stopped. My throat had tightened up again. What if Baba was seriously hurt, or even . . . How would we ever manage without him?

Uncle Hassan looked down at me again.

'*Inshallah* he'll be all right, Safiya. Look, we're at the hospital. We'll be with him in a few minutes.'

He was already turning in through the gates. I took a deep breath. There was a confession I had to make.

'Actually, Uncle Hassan, Baba will be really surprised to see you. He thinks you're still in America.'

'What? I don't understand! How did you know we were here? How did you get my address?'

We were at the front door of the hospital. I'd find out any moment now if Baba was alive or . . .

'Please, Uncle, can I tell you later? And could you let me out here?' I begged him. 'I can't bear to wait any longer.'

He hesitated, then nodded.

'All right. Go in through the main entrance and give your father's name to the reception desk. They'll tell you where to go. I'll come as soon as I've parked the car.'

CHAPTER FORTY-FIVE

I'm not used to hospitals. I should thank Allah for that, I suppose. The Al Bashir looked enormous and its bright white walls were so dazzling in the winter sun that I almost had to shade my eyes as I looked for the entrance. Inside, everything was cool and modern, but the super-clean hospital smell gave me the shivers. Had I come too late? Would Baba be . . . I couldn't even think the word.

I must have looked small and lost, standing there in the entrance, because a woman in a white coat paused as she rushed past and asked me if I was looking for someone. She passed me on to someone else and at last, after walking for miles down endless long corridors, I was standing beside a kind of trolley bed, and there was Baba, lying on his back, his eyes closed, a bandage half covering his head. His face was deathly pale.

I leaned over him.

'Baba! Open your eyes! Please, Baba, don't be dead. Baba!'

His eyes flickered open. He winced as he turned his head to look at me.

'Safiya! *Alhamdulillah!* Thank God you're all right. How did you get here? I've been so worried!'

The relief of hearing his voice made me almost dizzy. I touched his hand gently, afraid of hurting him.

'I – don't be angry, Baba – I . . .'

His eyes moved past me and opened in astonishment. I looked round to see that Uncle Hassan had come silently up behind me. He pulled up a chair and sat down beside the bed.

'Hassan? Am I dreaming?' Baba said, in a faint voice. 'What are you doing here?' He moved his head painfully in an effort to see past him. 'Where's Saba? Is she with you? Why aren't you in America?'

'We've been here for a while,' Uncle Hassan said gently. 'Adnan, I had no idea of the trouble you've been in, or even that you were here in Jordan. I thought you were in Damascus! I've been trying to contact you. No wonder I couldn't find you!' He turned to smile at me. 'Your remarkable daughter somehow knew we were here and had the good sense to come and find me.'

'What?' Baba frowned, as if the effort of understanding was painful. 'How did she . . .'

'I'll explain it all later,' I said hurriedly, desperate to stop him asking questions.

A nurse came in to check Baba's pulse and Uncle Hassan had to move out of the way.

'What do the doctors say?' he asked Baba when she'd gone.

'They want to do an X-ray, keep me here overnight for observation.' He spoke faintly, as if the effort was too much. 'They said it's severe concussion – I'm sure it's not that bad.'

I was doing sums in my head.

'Baba, how much will the hospital charge? Have you got Abu Mustapha's money? I've got about six JD in food money, and I can call Uncle Yasser and ask him—'

'None of this is necessary.' Baba was struggling to sit up. 'I'm perfectly all right. Safiya, bring my clothes. They're on that chair. We'll . . .'

Uncle Hassan put his hand on Baba's shoulder and gently pressed him down.

'Don't be ridiculous, Adnan. Safiya, stay here with your father and don't let him move. I'm going to sort things out.'

'Please, Hassan, there's no need . . .' began Baba.

'Frankly,' said Uncle Hassan, 'after all that's happened, it's the least I can do.'

Baba had closed his eyes again. I sat beside him, holding his hand, anxiously watching his face.

'Safiya,' he murmured, opening his eyes, 'you need to call Abu Mustapha. He doesn't know why I didn't come this morning. You'll have to explain. My phone's in my coat pocket.'

He waved a hand feebly towards a chair on which his clothes were heaped. I was relieved to have something to do.

The Hawk answered at once.

'*Na'am?* Yes?'

'This is Safiya, Abu Tariq's daughter,' I said in my best Perfumes of Paradise telephone voice. 'I'm afraid there's been an accident. My father was hit by a car on the way to his appointment with you. He's in Al Bashir hospital, awaiting treatment.'

Uncle Hassan had come. He watched me curiously while the Hawk talked into my ear.

'No, no, it's all right,' I said. 'My uncle's here. I'll call you with more news as soon as I know anything. Yes, I'll tell him. Thank you, sir. Al Bashir hospital. That's right.'

Uncle Hassan turned to Baba.

'Don't worry about anything,' he was saying. 'They're taking you for X-rays in a minute. You'll be staying in for as long as it takes to get you properly on your feet again.'

The fight went out of Baba. He smiled weakly with relief.

'And don't worry about Safiya. She's coming home with me,' Uncle Hassan said firmly.

My heart leaped with excitement at the thought of being with Saba, but plunged right down straight afterwards. What if Aunt Israa called me a beggar again? Would Saba turn on me too?

Baba had been drifting off to sleep but now his eyes flew open.

'Tariq,' he murmured. 'He'll be . . .'

I was still holding Baba's phone.

'I'll call Uncle Yasser,' I said. 'He'll tell Tariq and Uncle Malik. You mustn't worry, Baba.'

'I'll bring Safiya back later this evening,' Uncle Hassan said. 'Here come the medics, Adnan. You're in good hands now.'

CHAPTER FORTY-SIX

Back in the car park, I looked at my reflection in the dark, tinted window of Uncle Hassan's car while he called Aunt Israa.

I looked horrible! The rash on my face was a hideous red stain, my trousers were almost worn out and my shoes were only fit for the dump. No wonder Aunt Israa had called me a beggar.

'Uncle Hassan,' I said over the car roof. 'It's very kind of you, but I'd rather not come, if you don't mind. Aunt Israa will be upset. She thought I was . . .'

He frowned.

'Just get in, Safiya. I heard what your aunt said. She was in a panic. She didn't mean it.'

But I was the one in a panic now.

'Couldn't you take me to the bus station? I'd like to go back to Azraq. I'll be quite safe. Please, Uncle.'

He came round to my side of the car, opened the door and gently pushed me into the passenger seat. Then he got into the driving seat beside me, and turned to face me without switching on the engine.

'Listen, Safiya. You're coming home with me.' I was

shaking my head vigorously. 'No arguing. I want you to understand. Your Aunt Israa . . .'

'I know. Baba told me. She desperately wanted a baby, and when my mother came with Saba . . .'

'Don't interrupt. Your aunt is — she's a nervous person. She's easily upset. Israa has thought of no one and nothing except for Saba for the last thirteen years. She has protected her from every bump, scratch, disappointment and challenge since she was a tiny baby.'

'I do understand, Uncle Hassan. That's why I really, really think it would be best for you to—'

He smiled.

'You don't understand at all, my dear. And I can see that you're as obstinate as your twin, although I suspect you're rather better behaved. I must warn you that she might not react well at first when we tell her the truth.' He sighed. 'We should have told her years ago! I always knew it was wrong to let her think . . .' He leaned forward and turned the key in the ignition. 'I'm afraid,' he went on, inching the car forward out of the parking space, 'that Saba is hopelessly spoiled and self-centred. As a matter of fact, I think you're exactly what she needs.'

The journey to the hospital had seemed to take forever because I'd been so worried about Baba, but the drive back to Uncle Hassan's flat passed in a flash. I didn't want to arrive.

We had turned off the main road and were driving up the hill into the quiet back streets when Uncle Hassan suddenly said, 'So how *did* you know we were in Amman, Safiya? And how did you get hold of our address?'

I'd been waiting for this. I'd tried out several explanations in my head, each one sillier than the next, but now that the moment had come there was only one way to go. I had to tell the truth. I stole a sideways glance at him. There was something familiar about his face.

It's his eyebrows, I thought. *They swoop up in the middle, like Tariq's.*

The eyebrows made me feel better. Uncle Hassan was family, after all.

'It was before Baba explained – before he said that he didn't want us to try to meet Saba,' I began. 'I couldn't believe he really meant it.'

I stopped.

'Go on.'

'I was so desperate to find her! I've really missed my best friend, Farah, and I kept thinking about Saba, that she was just like me and we'd be closer even than friends! It was an accident finding out that you were here. Uncle Yasser caught sight of you going into the Askil building. Till then, I'd thought you were in America.'

We were nearly at the flats. I needed to hurry up.

'Anyway, I managed to go online at Perfumes of Paradise . . .'

'Perfumes of Paradise?'

'It's a beauty salon in Azraq. I've been working there, doing the accounts and being the receptionist.' I glanced at him again. He was drumming his fingers on the steering wheel. 'I liked being there,' I went defensively. 'I was good at maths at school. Doing the accounts – it was using my brain a bit. Better than nothing, anyway. And I got paid one JD for every day I worked there.'

'One JD. I see.'

He looked angry again, but I had no choice but to blunder on.

'Anyway, I looked up Askil, and found the phone number for Amman. Then I phoned up and persuaded the receptionist to give me your address.'

He drew in his breath sharply.

'She should have done no such thing. Do you know her name? That's a serious breach of security!'

'Oh no, please, Uncle Hassan, don't get her into trouble! She didn't want to tell me. She tried not to, really she did, but I – persuaded her.'

'How on earth did you do that?'

'I told her I was a florist. From Blossoms of Paradise.'

'I've never heard of them.'

'No, well, I made them up. I told her I had a big flower order for your daughter's birthday, and it would be a pity if she didn't get them. She only gave in when I said her name was Saba, as if I really knew the family.'

To my relief, he burst out laughing.

'*Wallah*, Safiya, until this moment I never realized how much I missed my sister. That's exactly what she would have done. She was a firebrand, just like you.'

'Was she, Uncle Hassan?' I suddenly felt wistful. 'Will you tell me about her? Baba never says anything. He can't bear to talk about her. If we ever mention her, he just gets sad.'

He had driven down the ramp into the underground car park beneath the flats by now, and was reversing into a space. He switched off the engine and even though the light was dim, after the brilliant sunshine outside, I could see that he was smiling.

'I'll tell you as much as I can,' he said. 'She was a wonderful, wonderful person. Come on now, *habibti*. We're home. No, don't look so nervous. You have courage enough for anything – I can tell.'

CHAPTER FORTY-SEVEN

It was all very well Uncle Hassan telling me not to be nervous, but how I could I help it? My heart was thudding as I followed him up the broad flight of pink marble-paved stairs to the landing.

As soon as we'd stepped into the flat, Aunt Israa fluttered out of a side room. Her eyes slid past me and fixed on Uncle Hassan.

'Is she ready?' Uncle Hassan asked brusquely.

'No. She doesn't feel like going out. She wants . . .'

'I don't care what she wants.'

He marched along the short corridor and thrust open a door at the end. I caught a glimpse of Saba lying on a bed, a headset clamped to her ears. Uncle Hassan bent down and pulled them off.

'Get up,' he said.

Saba jumped up and tried to snatch them back.

'Stop it! What are you doing?'

Uncle Hassan held the earphones out of reach.

'You're coming with me now,' he barked. 'Put your coat on.'

There was a nervous cough behind me.

'Please come in here,' Aunt Israa said.

She opened a door and almost pushed me into a sitting room. Two sofas were arranged opposite each other with a large coffee table in between them. A huge TV screen hung on the wall.

'Sit down, er – Safiya,' she said. 'I expect you're hungry. I'll get you something to eat.'

She's only offering because she thinks I'm a refugee beggar, I thought. *I'll show her.*

'No thanks, Aunt Israa,' I said, though I'd eaten almost nothing all day.

I could hear Uncle Hassan and Saba out in the corridor now, still arguing.

'Get your coat on *now*,' Uncle Hassan was saying.

'That's not the way to handle her,' Aunt Israa muttered. She hurried to the door and went out into the corridor. I heard her say, 'Your Baba will buy you an ice cream, my princess, at your favourite café.' She sounded as if she was speaking to a toddler.

'I don't want an ice cream,' snarled Saba. 'Why can't people just leave me alone?' Through the open door, her eyes met mine. 'And what's that beggar girl doing here again?'

Uncle Hassan snapped the door shut. I heard him say, 'For once in your life, you're going to do as you're told, Saba. There's something I have to tell you. I didn't want it to happen like this, but now it has.'

'What do you want to tell me? Why can't you do it

here?' Saba sounded sulky now, rather than rebellious. 'If it's about going to Dubai . . .'

'It's got nothing to do with Dubai. Here's your coat. Put it on.'

At last the front door shut behind them and their voices faded down the stairs.

I sat on the sofa, stiff with shock, my hands clasped tightly together. I'd never heard anyone talk to their father like Saba had done, except in foreign soap operas. A Syrian father would never have stood for it and a Syrian daughter would never have dared.

She's horrible! I thought, remembering the cold disgust in her eyes when she'd looked at me. *She's rude and mean and I don't like her at all!*

Where was the twin I'd been longing for, my soulmate, my long-lost sister? My dreams had once again shattered like broken glass.

Aunt Israa came back into the room. She was pale and shaking so much that I thought she was going to fall over, but I was too disappointed and upset to feel sorry for her.

'Look, Aunt Israa, I shouldn't have come,' I said defensively. 'But what else could I do? They took Baba away in an ambulance, and I was just left there, on the street, and this woman asked if I had any relatives in Amman and, well, you're the only ones, and I was so frightened. I didn't know what had happened to Baba, so I let her bring me here.'

She didn't seem to be listening.

'I'll go away,' I said. 'I'll go back to the hospital and sleep in a chair beside Baba's bed. I honestly didn't want to upset everyone.'

She took a tissue out of her pocket and wiped her eyes.

'No, no, Hassan wants – he says you ought to stay. I knew this would happen one day. He's been telling me for years that Saba ought to know everything, but I was so afraid she'd turn against me – against us!'

I shook my head.

'I'm sure she wouldn't do that.'

'No, but she might! She might want to leave me and go and live with you, and . . . and . . .'

She was crying again.

'Live with us?' I almost felt like laughing. 'I don't think so. We live in a tent. I can't even go to school any more.'

Her hand flew to her throat.

'In a tent? Oh, how awful! Saba wouldn't like that at all. I've always made sure she had the best of everything.'

She was starting to really upset me.

'We might be refugees, but we're not *beggars*,' I said, not even trying to keep the sharpness out of my voice.

She looked down.

'I shouldn't have said that. It was the shock. I knew who you were as soon as I saw you. You'd look exactly like her if it wasn't for the . . .'

The hideous rash all over my face and my crooked teeth, I wanted to say.

'I just wanted to get her away!' she went on. 'You don't

understand. She's very sensitive. You should have warned me you were coming.'

I couldn't believe my ears. Was she stupid, or what?

'How could I have warned you, Aunt?' I was trying hard to keep my temper. 'Baba had been taken away in an ambulance. I thought he was dead! Where else could I have gone? I was on my own. What could I have done?'

'Oh yes,' she said uncertainly. 'Oh, well, I suppose . . .'

This is where you're supposed to ask me how Baba is, I thought furiously.

But all she said was, 'I wonder how long they'll be? I hope Hassan's being gentle with her. Finding out that I'm not her real mother! She'll never get over it. I couldn't bear it if she turned against me!'

She dropped her head in her hands and her shoulders started to shake while I sat awkwardly beside her, not knowing what to do or say.

At last she looked up. She seemed almost surprised to see that I was still sitting there.

'I suppose I'd better make up a bed for you,' she said doubtfully.

'No, Aunt Israa, I can't stay here! Please, just call a taxi to take me to the hospital. I want to be with Baba.'

She shook her head.

'Hassan says you've got to stay.'

I hated the idea of being where I wasn't wanted, but it seemed as if I didn't have any choice.

Aunt Israa stood up.

'I'll do that bed,' she said.

I followed her out of the room.

'Let me do it. Just show me where to go.'

She looked surprised.

'You know how to make a bed?'

'Yes! Of course! Doesn't Saba?'

'I do everything for Saba,' she said defensively. 'Perhaps I should have taught her more practical things . . . encouraged her to be more . . .'

Her voice tailed away as she opened a door off the corridor into a tiny room without even a window, which had room only for a bed and a small table.

The maid's room, I thought.

There'd been one like it in our old flat in Damascus. Auntie Shirin had kept the vacuum cleaner in it. A moment later, Aunt Israa came back with a pile of bed linen and blankets. She dumped them on the bed and darted away again.

'I think I can hear them! Yes, they're back!'

She dashed out of the room. A key grated in the front-door lock. Quickly, I snapped the door of my tiny room shut.

'Oh, my heart, come to Mama!' I heard Aunt Israa say in a tearful voice.

Saba cut her off rudely.

'Have you got rid of her yet, my *so-called* twin?'

'My princess—' That was Aunt Israa again.

'Don't – touch – me,' stormed Saba, then her bedroom

door slammed so loudly that my own door shook.

My hand was on the door handle. This was the moment to tackle Uncle Hassan, but now he was talking to Aunt Israa. I strained to hear what they were saying.

'No, Israa! I won't hear of sending Safiya away on her own. Think what you're saying! A thirteen-year-old girl alone in a big hospital? Look, all these years I've given in to you about Saba. I knew it was wrong to keep the truth from her. I should have insisted. We should have tried harder to stay in touch with Adnan too. He's my brother-in-law! He's Saba's father!'

'He's not her father!' Aunt Israa almost screamed. 'You are, and I'm her mother!'

'All right. In every real sense, we're her true parents. She knows that, however much she kicks against it. We won't lose her. She needs us, now more than ever. But Safiya needs Saba too. And Adnan needs us badly. We're family, Israa! Family!'

I opened the door a crack and looked out. Aunt Israa's arms were flailing and she looked hysterical. Uncle Hassan was trying to hold her.

'Look at me, Israa!' he almost shouted. 'Don't you understand? We have to accept Safiya too.'

Aunt Israa slowly stopped struggling. Uncle Hassan dropped his hands as the fight seemed to go out of her. He glanced quickly towards my door, and pulled her into the sitting room, but I could still just hear what he was saying.

'We can learn to love Safiya.' His voice was gentler now. 'She's a remarkable girl. She's had to grow up much too fast, her education's been wrecked, she's living in a tent, cooking and caring for three grown men. She's lost her home, her wider family and all her friends. On top of that she's obviously been hideously exploited by some woman in a beauty salon who's been paying her one JD – one JD! – for a day's work.' He stopped. 'Israa, are you listening to me? Safiya will be a wonderful friend for Saba. She's the girl that Saba could become. Israa, have you heard a word I said? No, don't go to Saba. Give her time. She doesn't need you at the moment.'

But I could already hear Aunt Israa's slippers slapping on the marble tiles as she ran down the corridor. A door handle rattled.

'*Habibti*, open the door. Let me in. It's Mama!'

Then came a crash as if something had been hurled to the floor and smashed.

'You're not my mama!' Saba shrieked. 'Go away! I never want to see you again!'

Out in the corridor, Aunt Israa was wailing loudly. Another door opened and closed. The sound of her sobs and Uncle Hassan's quiet murmurings died away.

I sat down on the bed feeling awful. I'd upset everyone.

Even Uncle Hassan only wants me to stay because he thinks I might be good for Saba, I told myself. *She's all anyone cares about. No one cares about me. I hate her, anyway. I never want to see her again.*

I made a sudden decision.

I'll go right now. I'll find my way back to the hospital on my own.

I was still wearing my coat and my old white hijab, and my bag, which I'd been carrying around all day, was on the bed.

I opened the door of my room as quietly as I could. No one was in the corridor. I picked up my bag and tiptoed towards the front door, but just as I reached it Uncle Hassan came out.

'Safiya!' he said. 'No. Please.' Gently, he prised the handle of the bag out of my fingers and set it down. 'Don't run away. It's not the answer. Please.'

'I must, Uncle Hassan. Don't you see? I can only do more harm here. I just want to be at the hospital with Baba, and as soon as he's well enough I'll take him home to Azraq.'

'And it just so happens that I want to see him again too,' said Uncle Hassan, trying to sound cheerful. 'We'll go together. But, look, it's six o'clock already. You must be exhausted. I thought you'd like to take a shower and have something to eat before we leave. You don't want Baba to think you're not being properly looked after. The worry would set him back.'

I must admit that it wasn't the thought of Baba worrying that persuaded me. It was the magic word 'shower'. Hot water! Nice soap! Proper shampoo! The joy of washing myself all over without shivering and gasping with cold!

I let the bag go.

'All right. But I can't stay the night here. The hospital will let me sleep on the floor beside Baba. I'm sure they will.'

'We'll see about that later. There's the bathroom. Use whatever you find there. Take your time. We'll have something to eat when you're ready.'

That shower, in that clean, warm bathroom, was the greatest treat of my life. I lathered myself in a rich, sweet-smelling gel, shampooed and rinsed my hair till it squeaked, scrubbed the grime away from under my fingernails, then wrapped myself in an enormous, soft towel.

There was a hair dryer with a brush beside it, lying below the mirror. *Use whatever you find there*, Uncle Hassan had said. I'd take him at his word. I swept the brush through my long hair, feeling the knots untangle, and was about to switch on the dryer when someone tapped on the door. I opened it a crack. Aunt Israa stood there, holding some clothes out to me. Her eyes were down as if she couldn't bear to look at me.

'Hassan said – you needed some clean clothes.'

I wasn't ready for this.

'Are they Saba's?'

'No. They're mine. Please take them, dear. I'm sorry. I haven't been very . . . You mustn't think . . . Look, give me yours. I'll wash them and they'll be ready for you tomorrow.'

Her eyes were swimming again. I didn't have the heart to refuse.

'Thank you, Aunt Israa,' I said, and smiled.

At last she looked up at me.

'Oh!' She took a step back. 'You're exactly like her! With your hair loose and everything I can see you properly now. It's – it's extraordinary. Please, *habibti*, come and eat with us.'

'Is Saba . . . ?'

'No. I'll take her something later.'

I'd forgotten what it felt like to eat at a table in the western style, rather than round a cloth on the floor as I'd learned to do in Azraq. I was suddenly starving, and I couldn't wait to dive into the delicious food that Aunt Israa had magicked out of her fridge. Aunt Israa didn't sit with us. She bobbed back and forth, bringing more dishes and clearing away the ones we'd finished.

'Please, Aunt, eat with us,' I kept saying.

'I'll eat with Saba later,' was all she'd reply.

'Time to get going,' said Uncle Hassan at last. 'Are you ready, Safiya?'

I jumped up eagerly and went to fetch my coat. My crumpled hijab had been lying on top of it, but it had gone, and Aunt Israa had left a clean, nicely ironed one on my bed.

I was putting it on when the door burst open and Saba stormed in, brandishing a hairbrush.

'How dare you barge in here like this? Into my home?

Use *my* special shampoo and *my* hairbrush? Your dirty hair's all tangled up in it. My God, you're even wearing my mother's clothes!'

She raised the hairbrush. I thought she was going to hit me with it and backed away. My knees hit the edge of the bed and I collapsed on to it. She stood over me, her hands on her hips.

'I suppose you must be some relation or other, since you look so like me, but if you think I believe all this stuff about twins you must take me for an idiot. It's a trick, isn't it? A fraud. You're out for what you can get. I know you Syrian beggars. I see you everywhere round town. You people are all the same. Why don't you go back where you came from? No one wants you here, least of all *me*.'

I leaped to my feet.

'That's exactly what I'm going to do,' I said. 'Go back to where I came from. I can't wait to get away from you. I've been such a fool, believing that you'd be like my other self! I've dreamed about you loads of times, even talked to you in my head. All my life I felt that a part of me was missing, and that part was you.' A quick frown creased her forehead and her eyes flickered. 'Now I wish I'd never set eyes on you. You're a spoiled baby, Saba Adnan, and I'm ashamed to be your twin.'

She recoiled as if I'd hit her.

'I'm *not* Saba Adnan. Don't you dare call me that! I'm Saba Hassan, and you know it perfectly well.'

I pushed her out of the way and opened the door.

'Call yourself what you like. I couldn't care less. I'm going to the hospital to see my – *our* – father.'

'Then I'm coming too.' She followed me out into the corridor. 'I'm going to get the truth out of this fraudster, whoever he is.'

I gasped.

'Fraudster? You're calling our father a *fraudster*? You want to go and shout at him, in his hospital bed? How selfish are you? Baba's got a serious head injury! He needs peace and quiet! But you couldn't care less about him. You only care about yourself!'

Uncle Hassan came out into the corridor, his car keys in his hand. Saba ran up to him.

'Baba, take me to the hospital! I want to come too!'

She was whining like a little girl. I didn't wait for him to speak.

'You can want whatever you like,' I said, my voice full of disgust, 'but you're going nowhere near Baba until he's strong enough to stand the shock of finding out what kind of daughter he's got.' I paused, saw with satisfaction that this had hit home, and followed Uncle Hassan out of the flat. 'And when he does,' I added cruelly over my shoulder, 'he might never want to meet you at all.'

Uncle Hassan didn't say anything as we drove to the hospital.

He thinks I've been mean to Saba, I thought. But I was too angry to care.

Baba had been moved to a private room and we had to search the hospital for him all over again. We were in a lift, going to an upper floor, when Uncle Hassan cleared his throat and said, 'Safiya, I know you're angry, but try not to upset your father. He doesn't need an emotional scene just now.'

I didn't answer. How could Uncle Hassan think for one moment that I would be as selfish as my horrible twin?

We found Baba's room at last and stood looking through the glass panel in the door, not knowing if we ought to go in. He was lying on his back with his eyes shut and his mouth half open. Below the bandage round his head, huge purple bruises were beginning to show.

'You can go in,' a passing nurse said, 'but don't stay long. He's had some medication to help him sleep.'

I tiptoed up to the bed. Baba's eyes fluttered open.

'Safiya! *Habibti!* Are you . . . ?'

'I'm fine, Baba. Uncle Hassan's looking after me.'

'You've met . . .'

'Aunt Israa, yes. She's very kind.'

'Saba . . .'

'She's lovely, Baba. You mustn't worry about a thing.'

My voice was wooden, but he hadn't noticed. He closed his eyes. A smile of relief briefly lit his face, then faded.

'He's asleep,' said Uncle Hassan. 'Let's go.'

It was past nine o'clock by now and had been dark for hours. Although the headlights of oncoming cars lit up

Uncle Hassan's face in momentary flashes, I couldn't read his expression.

As we turned off the main road towards Um Uthania, he looked down at me with a smile.

'*Wallah*, Safiya, just think what an incredible series of chances has brought our family together again! There's nothing good to say about the terrible situation in Syria, but something wonderful has come out of it for us, at least.'

I wasn't ready for this. I didn't know how to answer.

'I expect you think I wasn't very nice to Saba,' I said at last, but so quietly that he had to lean over to hear me.

'She wasn't particularly nice to you,' he said dryly.

'The thing is, Uncle Hassan, I was angry and I . . .'

He turned briefly to look at me.

'Look, Safiya, none of this is your fault, but it's not Saba's either. Your aunt and I are the ones to blame. We all need to work to pull our family together again. I just hope that one day you'll see what a wonderful girl Saba really is — can be — and that you'll love her as much as I do. I think — in fact, I'm sure — that she's going to love you too.'

CHAPTER FORTY-EIGHT

The wonderfulness of Saba was the last thing on my mind as I trudged up the stairs to Uncle Hassan's flat. In my dreadful disappointment I'd closed my mind and heart to my long-lost twin. Anyway, I was totally exhausted and all I wanted was to climb into the cosy luxury of a real bed and go to sleep.

Saba's bedroom door was shut, but Aunt Israa had been hovering, waiting for us.

'I've put a nightdress on your bed,' she said, with a sideways look at Uncle Hassan as if she hoped for his approval. 'And a toothbrush. Do you want some hot milk, or anything to eat?'

'*La, shukran*, no thank you, Aunt,' I said, trying not to yawn.

A few minutes later, I was in bed, dressed in a soft, fluffy nightdress and was reaching for the light. But before I could switch it off, the door opened and Saba came in.

'All right,' she said. 'I accept that you're my twin and that I'm adopted.'

Reluctantly I dropped my hand off the light switch.

'Oh, do you. Good for you.'

'I suppose I was a bit . . .'

'Yes, you were.'

'It was the shock. I had no idea that . . .'

She'd flipped my angry switch again. No chance of going to sleep now. I sat bolt upright and glared at her.

'It was a shock. Poor you. Why does everyone go on about how important it is not to shock dear little Saba? I'll tell you about shocks. Try finding out that your father is wanted by the secret police. Try having to escape out of your country in the middle of the night on foot across a desert with people out there who want to shoot you. Try finding yourself living in a lousy smelly tent. Try not being able to go to school any more. Try finding your long-lost twin and discovering that she hates you and calls you a Syrian beggar. Try—'

'I don't hate you.'

We looked at each other for a long moment in silence.

'And I'm sorry I called you a beggar.'

Another silence.

'What do you mean, you live in a tent, and all that stuff about the desert?'

'Oh, never mind. Can I please go to sleep now? I'm really tired.'

'It was what you said,' she went on, as if I hadn't spoken, 'about always knowing there was someone else, someone you'd lost. I felt that too.'

Silence again.

'I was just so angry about being lied to! I mean, to find out that my mother was crazy and my father gave me away . . .'

'He didn't give you away. They lied to me just as much as they did to you. OK, our mother was sick, but she took you and left me. How do you think that makes me feel? Look, I really need to go to sleep, OK?'

'What's it like, where you live?'

'If I tell you, will you go away?'

'Yes.'

'Right. We're refugees. Poor Syrian *beggars*. We used to live in a beautiful flat in Damascus, much bigger than this one. Now we live in a tent. Tariq . . .'

'Who's Tariq?'

'My – our – brother.'

'I have a *brother*?'

'He's fifteen. He goes to school in the morning and works all afternoons, evening and weekends in a bottling plant. He earns 3JD a day and that's most of what we live on. I do all the cooking, washing, cleaning . . .'

'You live on three JD a day? You don't go to school?'

'No. There was no room for me in the school in Azraq. Anyway, we can't afford the fees.'

'That's so cool, having a big brother! Tell me about Tariq.'

'Not now! Don't you get it? I've been up since five o'clock this morning, I've walked miles in broken shoes that are two sizes too small, I've watched my father being horribly hurt in an accident, I've been called a beggar and a dirty refugee and my Baba's been called a fraudster. Now I just want some peace and quiet.'

'Oh!' She backed away towards the door. 'I'm sorry. Really. I didn't think.'

'No, you didn't.'

I'd had enough of Saba and, anyway, I couldn't keep my eyes open any longer. I switched off the light, turned my back on her and pulled the crisp clean sheet up around my neck.

I heard her say softly, 'Good night. Sleep well.'

Then I let the embrace of the soft warm bed carry me towards sleep.

CHAPTER FORTY-NINE

The next day was Friday. I hadn't slept so well since I'd been in my old bedroom at home. Perhaps it was the delicious comfort of the bed, the warmth, the soft pillow or the hushed quietness of Uncle Hassan's flat that confused me, but when I woke up at last I thought for a long moment that I really was at home in Damascus, that Auntie Shirin was in the kitchen making our Friday breakfast and that I'd have the whole day to relax, watch TV and hang out with Farah before we started helping each other with our homework.

Then I realized where I was. It was completely dark in my windowless room. I groped for the light switch and looked at my watch. Ten o'clock already! I needed the bathroom, and slipped out of my room.

No one was around, but from the kitchen I could hear the tinny crackle of music from a radio. I made it to the bathroom and back without anyone seeing me, quickly got dressed in the clothes Aunt Israa had given me, then sat on the bed, wondering what to do.

Yesterday, I'd just been in a disappointed rage with Saba, but now I was furiously jealous of her, and that was the worst feeling of all.

'She's got everything I've lost! It's so unfair!' I said out loud. 'I've got to get out of here, and forget we ever met.'

Aunt Israa knocked on the door.

'Come and eat your breakfast,' she said. 'Saba's at her piano lesson. She won't be back till twelve.'

Piano lessons for Princess Saba! I thought resentfully.

I followed Aunt Israa to the kitchen, but I couldn't eat much breakfast. All I could think of was how to get away. When I'd finished, I stood to help clear up the dishes.

Aunt Israa stopped me.

'No need to do that.' She put a pile of clean clothes – my clothes, which she'd washed and ironed – into my arms. Before I could thank her, she went on, 'Your shoes are too small for you, aren't they? I've looked out an old pair of Saba's. I suppose you're the same size.' She bent down to pick up a pair of trainers that had been tucked under my chair. 'She doesn't wear these any more,' she said. 'I thought you'd like to have them.'

Saba's cast-offs, I thought with disgust. I nearly refused them, but my feet were still so sore from yesterday that I couldn't bear the thought of forcing them into my horrible, small shoes again. I managed to say, 'Thank you, Aunt Israa. That's kind of you. Of her.'

Then I took the clothes and scuttled back to my room to get dressed.

A moment later, Aunt Israa knocked on the door and handed me Baba's phone.

'It was in your pocket,' she said. 'I nearly put it through the wash. Someone keeps trying to text you.'

I switched the phone on. There were dozens of texts, all from Tariq.

What's going on? Where's Baba? Where are you?

I felt awful. I hadn't let him know anything since that first phone call the day before.

If you've got Baba's phone, Safiya, for Allah's sake call me!

I scrolled through the rest of the messages.

Are you all right? Where are you?

Malik and I are on the bus from Azraq. Where is Baba?

I started trying to reply but there was too much to say for a text so I gave up and called instead.

Tariq answered at once.

'Baba? Is that you?'

There was a lot of background noise, rumbling and the sound of people talking.

'No, Tariq, it's me. I've got Baba's phone.'

'He gave you his phone? *Wallah!* He must be really badly hurt!'

'It's concussion. He's going to be all right. Where are you?'

'At the bus station. Just got here. Where is he?'

'Al Bashir hospital.'

'What? I can't hear you.'

'Al – Bash – ir – hos – pit – al.'

The line went dead.

I hurried back to the kitchen, feeling as relieved as a

lonely soldier whose comrades have arrived to help win the battle.

'Aunt Israa,' I said, 'I really need to get to the hospital. Can you call a taxi for me? I – I can pay.'

She looked horrified.

'A taxi? On your own? No, no, I'd never let Saba . . .'

'I'm used to it,' I said. 'In Azraq I go in a taxi on my own all the time.'

She looked disapproving.

'Hassan wouldn't like it at all.'

'Anyway,' I said cunningly, 'I'm sure it'll be nicer for Saba to have you to herself for the rest of the day. I mean, after the *shock* she's had . . .'

Her face lit up, then she had the decency to look a bit guilty.

'That's kind of you, Safiya. I need to help her come to terms with . . . It's been such a – such a surprise for all of us. I'll make up some little treats for her and . . .'

'And you'll call a taxi for me?'

'All right, dear. If you're sure.'

She was already reaching into her pocket for her phone.

I allowed myself one last lingering moment in the bathroom before I left, putting Dr Hannan's lotions on my rash, which was looking better already, then I washed my hands in the lovely scented soap and worked sweet smelling hand cream into them.

The taxi was waiting when I came out. Aunt Israa was clearly eager to see me go. She embraced me politely, but without affection, and had shut the front door before I'd got to the top of the stairs.

CHAPTER FIFTY

It took me ages to find Baba's room again in that huge confusing hospital, and when I got there at last I found Tariq and Malik standing beside his bed. I rushed at Tariq and flung my arms round him.

'I'm sorry I didn't call back sooner! It's been so – I was so . . .'

I was afraid he'd be angry, but he wasn't. He held me away so that he could look down into my face.

'Are you all right? You weren't hurt too?'

He looked so worried that I wanted to hug him all over again, but Baba called me, so I went over to the bed.

He was half sitting up and looked much better. The bandage round his head had gone. A patch of his hair had been shaved off and there were ugly black stitches holding together a short wound.

I bent to kiss him.

'Oh, Baba! Are you all right? Does it hurt much?'

'Just a bit of a headache. Where's Hassan?'

'Taking Saba to her piano lesson. He's coming later. Aunt Israa sent me with her own special driver.'

Don't ask me about Saba, I begged him silently. *Please*

*don't. And don't make me tell you that I came in a taxi on my
own.*

Malik came over to ask Baba something. Tariq was
tugging my sleeve, pulling me over to the window.

'How on earth did you get hold of Uncle Hassan?'

'I'll tell you later. Look, when are you going back to
Azraq?'

'I'll wait till Baba's discharged and go back with him.
But Uncle Hassan . . . ?'

'I said I'd tell you later. How long is Malik staying?'

'He's going back this afternoon. On the bus.'

I shut my eyes.

'Alhamdulillah! I'm going with him.'

'What? Why? Baba said you're staying with Uncle
Hassan. What's he like? What's Saba like? I can't wait to
meet them!'

I made a face.

'He's nice, I suppose. You'll like him, but Saba – oh,
Tariq, she's awful! She's totally spoiled and selfish! She
thought I was a beggar! She said "Syrian" and "refugee" as
if they were insults! She's mean and totally self-centred
and I hate her!'

Tariq whistled.

'Calm down, Safiya. Think about it. She'd had a shock,
that's all.'

'If,' I said dangerously, 'one more person tells me that
poor little Saba has been hateful to me because she's had
a shock, I'll – I'll . . .'

He grinned.

'All right, Miss Volcano. I get it. You've had a shock too, but there's no need to erupt all over me.'

'Don't you see, Tariq?' My voice started wobbling. 'I can't take this any more. I feel broken up inside. I've got to get away! If you can stay and look after Baba, I'll creep off with Malik, and I won't even have to say goodbye to her. To them.'

He nodded.

'If that's how you feel.' He gave me a playful punch on the arm. 'I've been really worried about you, you know, but you've been brilliant, getting hold of Uncle Hassan like that. I can't wait to hear how you did it.'

'It's a long story. I will tell you soon, I promise.'

In my pocket, Baba's phone buzzed.

'It's Uncle Hassan,' I mouthed to Tariq, and put the phone to my ear.

Tariq leaned in annoyingly close, trying to listen, and I had to push him away. My hands were shaking as I put the phone back in my pocket.

'He'll be here any minute,' I said, looking around wildly. 'With Saba. They're already at the hospital!'

Tariq put up a hand to ruffle the back of his thick thatch of hair as he always did when he was excited.

'That's kind of – interesting,' he said, trying and failing to look cool, as if he didn't care about meeting his sister for the first time since he'd been a toddler.

My stomach was curdling.

She's going to pretend to be sweet and nice and he's going to love her, I thought. *Baba will too. They'll end up wishing they had her instead of me.*

I set off blindly down the corridor.

'Where are you going?' Tariq called after me.

'Anywhere!' I called back. 'Anywhere you're all not!'

The lift ahead of me was whirring and the panel above it showed that it had already reached the second floor. Two more floors to go and they might be here. In a blind panic, I opened the nearest door and darted inside.

I found myself in a small, empty consulting room with a desk and chair for a doctor and another chair for a patient. I could hear the ping as the lift doors opened. Very carefully, I peered out through the glass panel in the door. Uncle Hassan and Saba were walking quickly past. He had his arm round her. Her hair was falling in long glossy waves round her face, and she was wearing a tightly cut jacket. A smart leather bag swung from her shoulder. I caught sight of her face. She looked scared and excited.

When they'd gone, I sank down into the patient's chair and screwed my hands together.

Let them all have a happy family reunion, I thought. *See if I care. They won't even notice I'm not there. They'll fall for her and think she's wonderful, but she doesn't fool me.*

I don't know how long I sat there. Time passed very slowly. I dreaded that the door would open and a doctor would come in and demand to know what I was doing there. I braced myself every time I heard someone hurrying down the corridor. Once Malik and Tariq walked past.

'And you've got no idea where she went?' Malik was saying.

'No!' Tariq answered. 'She just bolted.'

I didn't hear Malik's reply.

It was probably no more than half an hour, but it seemed like ages before at last I heard a man's heavy tread and a girl's lighter steps beside him. I opened the door a crack. Uncle Hassan and Saba had already gone past. I heard Saba say, 'I don't know why she had to run away like that,' and Uncle Hassan reply, 'None of this is easy for her, you know. Just think what she's been through.'

Saba's shoulders rose and fell in a shrug.

'I know, but she's so angry, and . . .'

Her voice faded as they stepped into the lift.

I waited till I was quite sure they'd really gone, then I walked slowly back to Baba's room, feeling defensive and a bit silly.

Tariq and Malik were standing by Baba's bed.

'It's so amazing meeting her!' I heard Tariq say. 'She's really cute, isn't she? Looks just like Safiya, but a whole lot younger. She's just a kid!'

He saw me and came over.

'Why did you run off? You missed the great family reunion.'

He was pretending to be cool but I could tell he wasn't

feeling it. I went over to the bed. Baba looked exhausted, and his eyes were wet with tears.

'So now you've met your other self,' he said in a shaky voice. He picked up my hand and squeezed it. 'You brought her back to me, *habibti*, and I'm so proud of you. You and Saba are going to be dearest friends, I know you are.'

He didn't seem to have noticed that I hadn't been there. I had to turn away to hide how hurt I felt.

A nurse came in with lunch for him on a tray. She put it on the table by the window and pulled a chair up for him.

'The doctor says you can get up,' she said.

Tariq and Malik tried to help him get out of bed, but he waved them away.

'I can manage fine,' he said.

I could see that he meant it. He walked quite strongly to the chair, sat down and pulled the table towards him. The meal smelled delicious – a fresh salad, meatballs in tomato sauce and freshly baked bread.

He picked up the flap of bread and was about to tear it when he noticed us watching him as we sat perched on the side of his bed. He pushed the table towards us.

'There's too much for me. We'll share it,' he said.

'No, no!' Tariq bent down to pick up his backpack from the floor beside the bed. 'Aunt Zainab gave us food to bring with us.'

Triumphantly, he produced some plastic containers

full of falafel and salted cheese, then, with a guilty look at me, he pulled out a blue plastic bag.

'Oh dear,' he said, 'they've got a bit squashed.'

I took the bag from him and looked inside.

'Abu Ali's cakes!' I said. 'He gave them to you, didn't he? Said they were stale and he couldn't sell them and his chickens were tired of eating them?'

'Well – yes. It seemed sort of rude to refuse. I couldn't say no.'

He caught my eye and we both burst out laughing. Suddenly, I felt much better.

Saba can't share any of this, I thought. *She'll never take away everything we've been through together.*

'It's all a bit weird, isn't it?' said Tariq, echoing my thoughts. 'I mean Saba won't ever be able to know us as well as we know each other. And she seems so young! You're really grown-up compared to her.'

I bent my head over my cake to hide how relieved I was. Saba wouldn't be able to take him away, however 'cute' she was. I'd be his first, real sister, whatever happened.

When we'd finished eating, Baba stood up, holding the back of the chair for support.

'I'd like to sleep now,' he said. 'Why don't you three go for a walk? Amman's a beautiful city. This is your chance to explore.'

Malik shook his head.

'I'm heading back to Azraq, Adnan. I've got a job fixed

up for tomorrow. I only came to be with Tariq and check how you were getting on.'

I stepped forward.

'And I'm going with Uncle Malik, Baba.'

He looked surprised.

'Really, *habibti*? Already? But you've only just met Saba. Don't you want to be with her? Why don't you stay?'

I hadn't properly prepared for this.

'I just think – Saba needs a bit more time,' I said lamely. 'To get used to everything.'

'That's my Safiya,' he said warmly, 'thoughtful for everyone else, as you always are.'

I bit my lip guiltily.

'Tariq's going to stay with you,' I said. 'He'll help you get back to Azraq when they let you out of here.'

'The day after tomorrow, I think,' Baba said, heading back to the bed. 'I'm really fine now. All I need is to be quiet for a while and rest. I want to leave as soon as I can. I can't bear to think what Hassan is paying for all this.' He turned to Tariq. 'Where are you staying tonight?'

'With Uncle Hassan,' Tariq said, avoiding my eye.

Baba yawned.

'That's good.

'We'll let you sleep, Adnan,' said Malik, stepping away from the bed. '*Allah yeshfeek*. May God keep you well.'

'*Inshallah*,' said Baba.

I followed Tariq and Malik out of the room, and we stood together in the corridor.

'Are you sure about this, Safiya?' said Malik. 'I thought you were longing to get to know Saba. Why do you want to rush away?'

'It didn't work out,' I said shortly. 'I don't want to talk about it. I just want to get out of here and go home.'

It was the first time I'd called the tent home. Tariq winced at the word.

'Some home,' he said gloomily.

'It's what we've got,' Malik said, 'and it's not that bad. When the winter's over, it'll be better.'

'Come on,' said Tariq. 'I'll walk to the bus station with you.'

The phone in my pocket buzzed. I handed it to Tariq.

'I forgot to give it back to Baba,' I said. 'You'd better take it back to him now.'

Tariq looked at the screen.

'It's a message for you. From Saba.'

'Delete it,' I said. 'Come on. Let's go.'

CHAPTER FIFTY-ONE

Malik and I hardly said a word to each other as the bus trundled eastwards out of Amman, into the cold, bleak desert region of Azraq. He spent most of the time, anyway, scrolling through his new phone.

'How much did you pay for that?' I asked.

He laughed.

'Nothing. I did a job for the guy in the phone shop. It's an old one but it's nice. Look.'

He passed it to me. I looked at it briefly and gave it back. Maybe, one day, I'd have a phone of my own again. In the meantime, I wasn't interested in Malik's.

It was dark when we got back to Azraq. I'd been so tired on that long bus ride back from Amman that I'd dozed most of the way. Saba, Uncle Hassan, Aunt Israa and Baba had danced through my head in a strange, surreal whirl. The walk from the town to the tent seemed endless and I had to admit I was glad to be wearing Saba's old shoes, which fitted me perfectly.

A light was on in Uncle Yasser's house. He must have been listening out for us, because as soon as I opened our gate he heard the hinges squeak and came running out.

'How is Adnan? I've been so worried! Those crazy drivers in Amman! So dangerous! Tariq called to tell us the news. He said it was only concussion, but you never know with head injuries!'

He looked really upset. I wanted to hug him.

'He's going to be all right, honestly, Uncle Yasser,' I said. 'He'll be home in a day or two.'

'*Alhamdulillah!* But, Safiya, how did you manage? Where did you go? On your own, like that, in a strange city! I haven't been able to put you out of my mind!'

I'd dreaded this moment. I'd have to tell him how deceitful I'd been. There was no keeping anything secret now.

'You must come and tell us all about it,' he went on. 'Zainab has cooked one of her lovely dinners. We can't let you go to bed without having a proper meal.'

'Thank you, Uncle,' I began, 'but . . .'

'It's very kind of Um Fares,' Malik interrupted firmly, taking me by the elbow and steering me towards the house.

'You might as well get it over with,' he whispered. 'Anyway, aren't you hungry?'

And I had to admit that I was starving.

It was strange to find myself the centre of attention as we sat round the tablecloth to eat. Aunt Zainab didn't approve of girls pushing themselves forward, and had always frowned at me when I'd tried to say anything with Uncle Yasser and Baba around. Anyway, I'd been pricked so often by her sharp tongue that I'd learned it was best to keep my mouth shut. But Uncle Yasser wanted to hear everything from start to finish and wasn't going to let me leave out a single detail. First he kindly asked about my appointment with Dr Hannan.

'Fancy Amman doctors!' Aunt Zainab sniffed, before I even had time to draw breath. 'A waste of time. If you hadn't scratched that little rash . . .'

Uncle Yasser stopped her with a wave of his hand. I spun the story out for as long as I could while trying to think out what to say about Uncle Hassan and Saba. I went into every detail of the accident.

'You see?' Aunt Zainab said triumphantly. 'It's what I've always said. No common sense. Adnan's supposed to be a brilliant lawyer, but when it comes to simple things like hailing a taxi . . .'

'That's enough, Zainab!' Uncle Yasser said sharply. 'So what did you do next, Safiya? The ambulance took Adnan off to the hospital and you were left standing there in the street on your own?'

Malik sat eating quietly, his eyes on his food, while Lamia listened eagerly, looking from me to her mother and father as if she was trying to work out which side she should be on.

'I'd have got into the ambulance,' she said boastfully.

'I wouldn't have let anyone stop me. I wouldn't have let *my* Baba out of my sight.'

'Of course you wouldn't, my pearl,' said Aunt Zainab.

I refused to be put off.

'It all happened very quickly,' I went on. 'A woman – she was really kind – came and asked me if I knew anyone in Amman, then she called a taxi and went with me to – to my uncle's house.'

Now for it, I thought. *I'll just have to tell them the truth.*

I could see the first question hovering on Aunt Zainab's lips, but before she could get it out, Lamia said, 'You're not supposed to go off in cars with strangers. She might have been a kidnapper. She might have sold you to people traffickers. She might have *murdered* you.'

Malik laughed.

'It would have to be a brave kidnapper. Safiya would get the better of any of them.'

'So this woman who helped you out,' said Uncle Yasser. 'Who was she?'

'I don't know, Uncle,' I said. 'She was just walking past when the accident happened.'

He slapped his knee delightedly.

'There, you see? I'm always telling you. There are so many good people in the world! Allah sent this angel to you, Safiya, just when you needed her.'

'What I want to know,' cut in Aunt Zainab, 'is how long you've been in touch with this uncle of yours? If he's rich enough to pay for a private room in Al Bashir hospital, why hasn't he looked after you all this time instead of leaving you up here to live on charity and depend on the goodwill of distant cousins like Yasser and me?'

Malik retreated back into himself and sat motionless, and Lamia looked excited, as if she was watching a competition and had just seen her mother score a point. But Uncle Yasser turned on Aunt Zainab angrily.

'Don't talk like that! It was Allah who brought Adnan and his family to us, as you know very well. I'm proud of all of you, how hard you work and how you try your best. I hope my family would do as well if we ever lost everything, like you did.'

Aunt Zainab flushed. She got to her feet and said stiffly, 'I've made some honey cakes. I'll bring them in.'

I saw her face as she stepped round me on the way to the kitchen. She looked ashamed.

'She speaks hastily,' Uncle Yasser said apologetically. 'You know your aunt. She regrets it afterwards. She's fond of you all, really. Now go on, Safiya. How did you manage to get hold of Hassan?'

I took my time over the story, and even enjoyed telling it. Sitting on the cushions, the remains of Aunt Zainab's delicious meal spread out on her pretty cloth on the floor, Uncle Yasser, Aunt Zainab, Lamia and Malik leaned forward and listened eagerly.

Every now and then someone interrupted.

'Typical!' Uncle Yasser said with disgust when I told them how I'd seen the story of Askil International's move to Dubai in the newspaper. 'Our economy's in a mess! Jobs and capital moving out of Jordan all the time!'

No one took any notice of him.

'What did you do next?' asked Lamia breathlessly.

I felt a bit guilty as I explained how I'd searched for Uncle Hassan on Um Khalid's computer.

'I don't suppose she'd be very pleased to know about *that*. Surfing the web in office time,' Aunt Zainab put in tartly, as she picked up another honey cake and put it on Lamia's plate.

I explained about the phone call to Askil International and how I'd pretended to be a florist from Blossoms of Paradise, and I even put on my best telephone voice to replay the conversation to them. Uncle Yasser and Malik shouted with laughter. Lamia said, 'You're so amazing, Safiya,' and even Aunt Zainab couldn't help smiling, before she made herself frown and say, 'I hope you don't think that trickery and lying are things a decent girl should do.'

Lamia kept badgering me to tell her more about Saba.

'What's she like? Did you meet her? Does she look exactly like you? I wish I had a twin. It's like a story in a book!'

'Yes, I did meet her and, yes, she looks like me. No, I don't know what she's like – I hardly saw her, so I didn't have time to get to know her,' I said shortly.

Luckily, before Lamia could pester me any further, Uncle Yasser stood up.

'It's late,' he said. 'Lamia, go to bed. The most important thing is that Adnan is in good hands and is getting better quickly. Also that Allah has kept our Safiya safe and brought her back to us. Malik, can you come over in the morning? I want to talk to you about a blocked drain in the bathroom.'

He went out of the room. Automatically I started clearing the plates off the floor.

'Well,' Aunt Zainab said, as I followed her into the kitchen, 'now that your father's doing business with his grand friend in Amman, and you've got hold of your rich uncle, I suppose you'll be going off to live in Amman yourselves. You won't be able to get away from Azraq fast enough. We'll be your poor relations again.'

There was no point in answering that. Anyway, I didn't know what to say. There was a note in Aunt Zainab's voice that I hadn't heard before. It sounded almost like respect. There was regret too, as if she'd actually be sorry to lose us. But I didn't want to think about Aunt Zainab. I was beginning to realize that escape routes were opening up, away from Azraq, away from the tent.

She put the tray she'd been carrying down on the kitchen table and wagged a finger at me.

'And remember this, Safiya, when you're back in your nice life, with everything laid on for you, that we were the ones who took you in. You'd have ended up in the gutter or a refugee camp if it hadn't been for us.'

Suddenly, weirdly, as I looked at Aunt Zainab's tired

face, the bitter lines etched round her mouth, and the look of disappointment in her eyes, I felt a rush of affection for her. In spite of all her jealousy and bitterness, her sharp digs and the harsh demands she'd made of me, she'd been there when I'd needed her. She'd looked out for me in her own rough way. I'd come to respect her and, although she tried to hide it, I knew she respected me too.

I'd rather have you than Aunt Israa, anyway, I thought.

Before I knew what I was doing, I'd put my arms round her and hugged her. She stiffened at first, as if she wanted to push me away, then she awkwardly patted me on the back.

'There's no need for that. Go off to bed, and kindly come back here tomorrow morning to help me clear all this up.'

CHAPTER FIFTY-TWO

I felt bad about myself when I woke up the next morning. Why had I yelled at Saba like that? I'd let myself down. I must have looked like a complete fool. It was always the same with me. I'd explode and upset everyone, but once I'd calmed down I'd feel ashamed and silly.

I know she was mean to me, I thought, *but I told her she was spoiled and selfish. She won't forgive me for that.*

I turned on to my back and looked up unseeingly at the thin slope of canvas, which was all that separated me from the freezing winter air outside.

I don't care, anyway, I thought. *I've just got to forget I ever met her, with her stupid piano lessons and braces on her teeth and fancy bedroom. It's nothing to do with me. Accept it, Safiya. You're on your own. That's just how it's going to be.*

I remembered how we'd glared at each other beside the gold-framed mirror beside Uncle Hassan's front door.

We must have looked a bit funny, I thought, *two identical faces yelling at each other. Saba's got a temper just like mine, only I bet Aunt Israa never punished her for it, not like Auntie Shirin used to punish me. She probably feels silly now too. Good.*

I hope she does. Let her think about someone else for a change, instead of her precious self.

I could hear Malik stirring. It was time to get up.

'It's turned colder,' he said as I went out of my room into the main tent. He was standing by the open flap, looking up at the heavy grey sky. 'Looks like snow's coming.'

I shivered. I'd loved snow when we'd been children. Damascus had looked magical, and Tariq and I had made snowmen in our courtyard, but there had been a warm flat to go back to and Auntie Shirin had made us hot drinks and dried our wet clothes. The thought of snow was scary now.

I got Malik his breakfast, fed Snowball, tidied up and went across to the house. For the first time ever, Aunt Zainab opened the door at once, almost as if she'd been waiting for me. I could see that she was dying to hear more about the family in Amman. My story would give her enough to gossip about for weeks.

'That Israa woman, whatever does she look like now?' she began as I started on the washing-up. 'When I saw her at your parents' wedding I knew she'd age badly.'

'She looks all right,' I said unwillingly. 'Just ordinary. I didn't notice.'

'You were too busy swooning over your precious twin, I suppose.'

'I hardly saw her,' I said shortly. 'She looks like me, but she's not the same as me at all.'

Aunt Zainab had been sorting out last night's leftovers in the crowded fridge. She shut the door and looked at me shrewdly.

'It must have been strange for you, Safiya. Not too easy, I suppose? I mean, she's got everything you haven't got. Goes to one of those smart expensive schools in Amman, nice clothes and all that? It would be easy to give in to jealousy. You need to watch out. No one likes a jealous person.'

You should know, I thought with a sniff.

'I expect you scared her,' she went on. 'You've grown up since you came to Jordan. You're a strong young woman now. Independent, capable. An excellent cook. You've left her miles behind, I'm sure.' And then she smiled at me, taking me completely by surprise.

I remembered suddenly how she'd said to her sister, *What she needs is* training. *She's got to learn in the school of hard knocks.* I wanted to say, *So I've graduated from your school now, have I? Got a certificate for me, Aunt Zainab?*

The weird thing was that I did actually feel grateful to her, and I was trying to think of a way to thank her when she gave in to the temptation to deflate me in her usual way. 'I wouldn't get your hopes up that your posh uncle will get you out of here,' she said. 'He'll be off to Dubai without a backwards glance.'

I had time to think about what she'd said as I helped around the house. Was I *a strong young woman*? Perhaps I was. Was it possible that Saba had been scared of me?

I could have been a bit nicer, I thought regretfully. *I've blown my chances now.*

And what did Aunt Zainab mean about Uncle Hassan getting us out of Azraq? He was going to live in Dubai. We wouldn't see him again for years.

It was early afternoon when, at last, I heard the creak of our compound gate.

'That'll be Uncle Malik,' I told Aunt Zainab. 'I need to go back and sort things out before Baba comes out of hospital.'

I'd almost forgotten now how scared I used to be of her. A few months ago, I'd never have dared talk to her so boldly. I was out of her house before she'd thought of an answer.

Malik was looking pleased with himself.

'Look what I've got,' he said, proudly displaying a large box sitting by the front tent pole. 'I carried it all the way back from town. It's so heavy I thought my arms would drop off.'

He was opening the box as he spoke.

'A heater, see? Works on kerosene. I applied to a refugee charity for it a few weeks ago. Didn't want to tell you in case I didn't get one.'

'Honestly, Uncle Malik, you are, you are . . .' I didn't know what to say. 'Like a wizard in a story,' I finished lamely.

'Adnan needs to be comfortable when he gets back,' he

said. 'Tariq's just texted me. The hospital's discharging him tomorrow morning, and that rich business friend of his, Abu Mustapha, is bringing them both up to Azraq in his car.'

'Tomorrow? The Hawk's driving him up himself? When will they get here?'

'Tariq didn't say.'

All I could think of was the almost empty trunk in the kitchen. The monthly food box wasn't due for another week, but I'd need to make a proper meal to celebrate Baba's return. A big menu started to unroll in my head.

I suppose Saba's gone to see Baba again today, I thought. *He's probably wishing I was as nice as she's making herself out to be. I'll show him. I'm sure she can't even make a pot of tea. I'll cook a dinner that he'll really enjoy.*

Malik was fiddling with the heater, pouring in some evil-smelling kerosene from a bottle.

'Let's see if it works,' he said, and lit the wick.

A delicious heat spread out from it. Almost at once, he turned it off it again. He picked up the kerosene bottle and made sure the cap was tightly screwed on.

'This stuff's expensive. We'll keep it for the evenings. We'll have to be really careful not to set everything on fire.'

I wasn't even listening.

Chicken in turmeric and yogurt sauce, I was thinking. *Stuffed cabbage leaves, if I can afford a bit of beef mince.*

'Please, Uncle Malik,' I said, 'I need to cook. Meat

and stuff from the butcher in town. Do you think . . .'

He didn't even let me finish.

'All right. I'll go. What exactly do you want?'

I was up early the next morning. Several finished dishes were already sitting on the bench in the tiny lean-to kitchen, protected from Snowball by plates with weights on top. I worked like a fury, sweeping, tidying, tucking blankets neatly round mattresses and arranging pillows artistically.

'When you haven't got much money, being clean and tidy is your luxury,' Aunt Zainab had said to me more than once. She'd irritated me at the time, but I was beginning to understand what she meant.

I'd just come back from Abu Ali's shop, where I'd gone to buy a few last-minute things, and was putting them down in the kitchen, when I heard a car draw up.

'They're here!' I called out to Malik, who had been clearing out the trench behind the tent again.

I ran to open the gate just as a few fat snowflakes started to fall.

The first person I saw was Tariq, leaping out of the back and running round to the front passenger seat to help Baba. But instead of the Hawk it was Uncle Hassan who got out next from behind the driving wheel. And then my heart missed a beat, because, after a long pause, the last person to appear was Saba.

CHAPTER FIFTY-THREE

I stood there, frozen with embarrassment as much as with cold. There was no hiding our poverty now.

At least I've made a nice meal, I thought, *and if you don't like it you can just go away again.*

Then I saw that Saba was scared. The dancing snowflakes falling between us blurred her face, but there was no mistaking the hunch of her shoulders and her hesitation as she stepped slowly towards me.

Tariq and Uncle Hassan were trying to take Baba's arms to help him through the gate. He shook them off.

'Really!' he objected. 'There's no need. I'm quite all right.'

Saba had reached me now.

'*Ahlan wa sahlan*, you are welcome,' I said, my voice sounding colder than I'd intended.

She flinched.

'Safiya, don't be angry any more. I'm sorry if you didn't want me to come. I wouldn't let my Baba call to warn you in case you refused to see me. I've been feeling so awful – I've been a total idiot. I just, I desperately wanted to see you again.'

The knot inside my chest loosened a little bit, but now I was confused, not sure what I was feeling.

'Look,' I said. 'The snow's settling on your hair. Let's go inside.'

I led the way into the tent. Malik had stayed behind to close the gate. He went forward to embrace Tariq and Baba, shook hands with Uncle Hassan, then he moved into a corner, making himself invisible, shy as he always was in company.

I couldn't bear the humiliation of watching Saba's face as she looked round the tent. I ran forward to hug Baba.

'Baba! Are you all right? Have you got a headache? How was the journey? What did the doctor say? Look, Uncle Malik's got us a heater.'

I was babbling stupidly but I couldn't stop myself.

Tariq was inspecting the heater.

'This is so cool,' he said.

'I hope not,' Malik said, almost too quietly for anyone to hear. 'It's supposed to be hot.' Everyone laughed and he blushed. 'I'll light it.'

Uncle Hassan, Baba and Tariq settled themselves on the mattresses while Malik lit the heater. We all watched him as if lighting a heater was the most interesting thing in the world. I still couldn't bring myself to look at Saba.

'I'll get the tea,' I said, escaping to the kitchen, but to my dismay, she followed me.

'What can I do to help?' she asked eagerly.

'There's a tray down there,' I said unwillingly, pointing

below the counter. 'You can put the tea glasses on it.' I
started filling the kettle from the drinking water bottle,
wondering why my hands were shaking. 'The sugar's
down there too.'

I watched out of the corner of my eye as she nervously
set the glasses on to the tray. Her hands were shaking too.
The sugar bowl slipped from them. She managed to catch
it, but some white grains fell on the counter and dissolved
at once in the drips of water I'd left there.

'Oh dear, I've made a mess,' she said. 'It's all sticky
now. I'll clear it up. Where's the tap?'

My stomach clenched.

'There isn't a tap. We don't have running water. The
bottle in here's just for drinking. There's a tank outside. I
fill the bucket from it.'

She jerked backwards nervously.

'Sorry. I didn't . . .'

'It's all right. Honestly. I'll clear it up later.'

There was an awkward silence.

'Are you . . .' I began.

'Do you . . .' she said at the same time.

We both laughed uneasily.

'I've forgotten what I was going to say, anyway,' she
said.

'So have I.'

I fetched out my best plate, one that Malik had
somehow picked up in Azraq. Suddenly it looked cheap,
with its fussy decoration of roses and bows.

'There are some cakes over there, in that plastic box,' I said. 'Could you put them out on this?'

'Yes, yes, of course.'

I had my back to her as I poured the boiling water into the teapot. I heard the lid of a container snap open.

'Oh,' she said, 'but this looks like a stew or something.'

I turned round. She'd opened the wrong box.

'That's for our dinner,' I told her.

'It smells lovely.' She was being too enthusiastic. 'Do you get your stuff delivered from a restaurant?'

I tried to suppress a laugh, but it came out anyway in a snort.

'On three JD a day? With some help from a box of charity food? No! I cook everything myself.'

Her hand, holding a cake above the plate, froze in mid-air.

'Oh my God, Safiya, I don't know what to say. You're so incredible. I just keep putting my big foot in it.'

She looked so contrite that the knot in my chest loosened a bit more.

'Honestly, it doesn't matter. You couldn't be expected to know what it's like for us here.'

'But I want to know everything!' she said earnestly. 'Since you told me you lived in a tent, I've been trying to imagine it. At home, in America, I mean, last summer, I went on a camping holiday. It was so fun! A bunch of us in tents, these crazy guys, and my best friend Melanie . . .' She was fumbling for the right words in Arabic as if the memory was making her think in English. 'I thought it would be a bit like that,' she finished lamely.

She was so sincere that I couldn't help smiling.

Anyway, I thought, *a year ago, in Syria, I couldn't have imagined all this either.*

'People used to camp for fun in Syria,' I told her. 'Foreign tourists, mainly. They'd go off into the desert with fancy tents and camels and pretend to be like the Bedouin. They'd make campfires and roast sheep and everything.'

Tariq stuck his head through the kitchen entrance.

'Are you to going to be all day in there? Where's our tea?'

He disappeared again.

'I'll take the tray,' I said, 'if you can take the cakes.'

She picked up the plate.

'Oh! Look!' she said.

'What?'

'Your thumbs.'

'What about them?'

'There's a ridge running down the middle of the nail, exactly like mine.'

It was freezing in the little kitchen, but it was the weirdness of our two unusual thumbs, mine on the tray, hers on the plate, that made me shiver.

I looked up and our eyes met.

'Safiya,' she begged, 'please, please be my friend. My sister. I need you so badly. You have no idea how much.'

CHAPTER FIFTY-FOUR

The early darkness of winter was falling by the time we'd finished our tea. We'd kept the tent flap open to give us light, though it meant that much of the warmth of the heater escaped outside.

At last, Tariq got up to shut it, but just before he let it fall something small swooped inside. He darted back. A little bird had flown in. It settled on top of the partition dividing my room from the rest of the tent. It looked dazed, fluffing out its feathers.

'You don't want that in here,' said Uncle Hassan, getting ready to jump up. 'I'll catch it.'

'No, no, let the poor thing be,' said Baba. 'It's half frozen. It's just looking for shelter. Make sure Snowball doesn't get it, Safiya.'

Snowball had crept in earlier, looked suspiciously at the strangers, then stretched out near the heater. Her purrs made everyone smile. Malik switched on the solar lamp and hung it from the tent pole. There hadn't been enough daylight to charge it fully, but it would shed a dim light for a few hours.

Tariq was still by the entrance, looking out into the twilight.

'The snow's settling,' he said.

Uncle Hassan looked worried.

'We ought to make a start back. The roads'll be icy soon. It'll be dangerous.'

Saba put on her spoiled child's pout.

'No! Not yet! I want to stay!'

Her voice came out in a whine. Baba's eyebrows twitched together in a frown. Tariq and Malik glanced at each other then looked away, embarrassed.

'You're very welcome to stay, of course, Hassan,' said Baba. 'I'm sure Yasser will put you up in the house tonight.'

'Yes! Yes! Ple-e-ase!' Saba insisted childishly. 'I want to stay with Safiya!'

Malik got up quietly. He came back a few seconds later.

'Excuse me, Abu Saba,' he said tentatively to Uncle Hassan, 'but it's coming down fast now. It'll be hard to drive through the snow in the dark.'

Uncle Hassan looked worried.

'Israa will be beside herself!'

'No, she won't!' said Saba loudly. 'Tell her I *want* to stay. Tell her—'

'That's enough, Saba,' said Uncle Hassan, turning on her sharply. 'You're not in America now, as I keep reminding you. Syrian children do not tell their parents what to do, make demands and show disrespect.'

Saba looked around, aware for the first time of the uncomfortable silence that had fallen. Everyone else was looking down, embarrassed. She went red. Her lips trembled and I could tell she was on the edge of tears.

Uncle Hassan stood up, went to the flap and looked out.

'Malik's right,' he said heavily. 'It's too late to go now. We'll have to stay the night.'

Saba tried to help me get the supper ready, but there was hardly room even for me in the tiny canvas kitchen, and she kept getting in my way. She gave up after a while and stood back to watch as I boiled the rice, heated the chicken stew and chopped herbs to sprinkle on top.

'You're like a grown-up,' she said suddenly. 'You make me feel stupid and ignorant. I'm just a baby compared with you.'

Something twisted inside me. I turned to look at her, the spoon I was holding dripping gravy into a saucepan.

'I don't want to be a grown-up!' I burst out. 'I don't want to have to do all this stuff! I want to be a normal girl and go to school! Have a mama to . . . to . . . look after me.'

'What was she like, do you think, our mother?' asked Saba, after an awkward pause.

'I wish I knew. I never used to think about her, but now I do all the time. Auntie Shirin, who brought us up, she was all right, I suppose, but she didn't seem to love us much, not like our real mother would have done.'

Saba looked away from me, frowning.

'I know you think I'm the lucky one,' she said, 'having a mama and everything, but honestly it's not that great. It sounds weird, but she loves me too much. It's like she's obsessed! She treats me like I'm still five years old. I'm thirteen!'

I pretended to look surprised.

'Really? Guess what? I'm thirteen too!'

She raised her eyebrows mockingly.

'Well now, there's a coincidence. Don't tell me your birthday's in November?'

'It is! The fourteenth!'

She started giggling, then I joined in and a moment later we were holding on to the counter, helpless with laughter.

Tariq put his head through the flap.

'What's the joke, sis? And – er – sis?'

'Nothing to do with you,' I said. 'Go away.'

He pulled a face.

'Ganging up on me already? I might have known it.'

He disappeared again.

Saba was still looking at the flap through which he'd disappeared.

'It's so amazing to have a big brother! Gorgeous, isn't he?'

'Gorgeous? Tariq? Are you serious? He can be a real

pain.' She looked doubtful. 'Wait till he starts bossing you around and being all grand and domineering.'

'I heard that!' Tariq's face appeared again. 'Saba, you're definitely, as of this moment, my favourite sister.' He must have seen the spike of anxiety in my eyes, because he added, 'No, wait. It's got to be Safiya because she's cooked an amazing dinner and if I'm not careful she won't give me any. Can't you hurry up with it? We're all starving in here.'

I fished under the counter and pulled out the cloth.

'It's ready. You can make yourself useful and lay this out.'

He pretended to bow.

'Yes, ma'am. In the dining room, I presume? With the best silver?'

'Of course. And the crystal glasses.'

Saba was looking delightedly from me to him and back again.

'You're so lucky,' she said with a sigh.

'Us? Lucky?' said Tariq. 'You have to be joking.'

'No, but you are,' said Saba. 'You've always had each other.'

CHAPTER FIFTY-FIVE

When I cook something I never know if it's all right or not until I've dished it up and everyone's started eating. But from the moment the food was on the plates I knew my meal was a triumph.

I sat back and watched as everyone enjoyed the food. Their faces, sitting in a ring round the bright tablecloth, were softly lit by the solar lamp and the glow of the heater. The reds, oranges and purples of the rugs, cushions and blankets glowed warmly. Malik had shooed Snowball out of the way, and she'd retreated reluctantly to her sleeping place by the flap. No one spoke much. Questions seemed to hang in the air that no one dared to ask.

'That was absolutely delicious, Safiya,' said Uncle Hassan, putting his plate down at last. 'Where did you learn to cook?'

'Trial and error,' Tariq said teasingly. 'Sometimes more error than trial.'

Saba sniggered, but Baba gave her a reproving look.

'Aunt Zainab taught me mostly,' I said. 'And I just sort of taught myself.'

'Aunt Zainab?' enquired Uncle Hassan.

'My cousin Yasser's wife,' explained Baba, 'which reminds me that we ought to go over and ask if they can give you both a bed for the night.'

Saba, sitting beside me, stiffened. She drew in her breath and the childish look settled on her face. Then she seemed to think, and said quietly, 'Baba!'

'Yes, Saba?' said Uncle Hassan.

'What is it, *habibti*?' Baba said at the same time.

Everyone laughed nervously.

'I meant Baba Hassan,' Saba said. 'Actually, I've thought about this and if you don't mind I'd like to go on calling you Baba. I mean, you've always been my Baba and always will be and I don't want to change that now.' Uncle Hassan grunted, and I could see that he was trying to hide how pleased he was. 'But,' Saba went on, turning to Baba with a charming smile, 'I thought I'd call you Baba Adnan, if that's all right.'

'That's perfect, *habibti*,' said Baba with a fond smile.

I felt a stab of jealousy. Saba was so charming! Was Baba falling under her spell?

'So what did you want to say?' asked Uncle Hassan.

'It's only – I just – please may I stay in the tent tonight?' Baba looked concerned.

'My dear, you have no idea. It's really not at all comfortable. The – the bathroom is hardly what you're used to you.'

'Safiya puts up with it so I'm sure I can,' Saba said, still keeping her voice low and polite. 'We can sort of curl up together, that is, if she wouldn't mind?'

She looked at me. I recoiled inside. My cold little room with its hard, narrow mattress hardly had room for me and, anyway, I wasn't sure if I was ready to be so close.

'You won't like it much, honestly,' I said awkwardly.

'I wouldn't mind anything,' she said, 'as long as we can be together.'

Her face as she looked at me was anxious and pleading. I could see she was really trying.

'All right,' I said unwillingly.

I got up to clear away the meal. Saba eagerly rushed to help me. Our movements seemed to wake the little bird who began to sing in a high, trilling voice. The sound was so unexpected that everyone laughed.

'Well, that seems to be settled,' said Uncle Hassan. 'And in fact, Adnan, there's no need to bother your cousin. I'm sure I can bed down here. Anyway, there's a great deal that I wish to discuss with you. There are only three weeks till we leave for Dubai. I'd like to get things settled.'

Tariq jumped up.

'You can have my mattress and blankets if you like, Uncle Hassan. Aunt Zainab will give me a bed. I'll take my books and everything and go straight to school in the morning.'

Saba nudged me.

'What's Aunt Zainab like?'

I pulled a face.

'Difficult. She doesn't like me much. Spoils Tariq all the time, though.'

'She sounds mean,' Saba said sympathetically.

'She is, and I can't say I like her exactly, but it's weird. I just sort of get her, if you see what I mean.' I paused. 'Actually,' I went on slowly, 'I hadn't really thought about it, but the truth is that she's helped me and looked after me when I've most needed her. She taught me to cook too.'

'I want you tell me about her, tell me *everything*,' Saba said earnestly. 'That's why I wanted to stay.'

In spite of myself, I felt a glow hover near my heart. All I had to do was let it in.

CHAPTER FIFTY-SIX

Before I met Saba, I'd imagined that talking to her would be like talking with myself, that we'd instinctively know each other's thoughts and share each other's feelings. It wasn't like that at all.

'Tell me everything,' Saba had demanded, but how could I, when there were so many things she didn't understand? What had she ever known about being poor and homeless, and looking after a family of men?

There was a gulf between us, and the bridge across it was shaky.

Haltingly, I told her how we'd had to leave Damascus in a hurry, leaving everything and everyone behind.

'I understand just how you felt!' she said eagerly. 'When we moved here from New York, I cried for days. Honestly.'

No, Saba, I thought. *You have no idea at all.*

But if I couldn't touch her with my mind, did I like curling up with her in my cold, narrow bed? I think I did. I wasn't used to being so close to another person, to feeling their warmth against me, and I lay rigidly at first, even after she'd fallen asleep. But after a while I relaxed, and then, I don't know why, I began to cry, muffling my breathing in case I woke her up.

I think I was crying for the girl I might have been. A girl like Saba, with a good life ahead of her, school, piano lessons and braces on her teeth. A girl with nice clothes, a bathroom and a phone. And I was crying for the girl I'd become, lonely, struggling to keep myself clean, my clothes old and worn, anxious every day about making ends meet, not daring to think about the future.

I just want to be thirteen again, I said to myself, over and over again.

After a while Saba turned over, dragging the blanket off me. I pulled it back, as gently as I could, but she woke up and said sleepily, 'Oh, sorry. Are you cold? Are you all right?'

No, I wanted to say. *Nothing's all right.*

But what I actually said was, 'Yes, I'm fine.'

Beyond the partition, Baba and Uncle Hassan's low voices still rose and fell. Uncle Hassan sounded insistent, but Baba seemed to be resisting him. Then I heard Uncle Hassan say clearly, 'But it would be the best thing for all of us, don't you see?'

Saba had woken up properly. She moved her head on the pillow and felt the wetness of my tears.

'Oh, Safiya! You've been crying. Was it me? Did I make you sad?'

'No,' I said gruffly. 'I'm all right. Just cold, as usual.'

In the dark she felt for my face and gently stroked my

cheek. Tears pricked my eyes again. This time I didn't try to hold them back.

'You've got everything I've lost!' I burst out. 'I know you don't want to go to Dubai, but you'll be able to go to school! Pass exams! One day you'll go to university and have a career. You've got a *future*!'

'Oh,' was all she could say. 'Safiya, I'm sorry. I . . .'

'Don't be sorry. It's not your fault. But look at me! All I am is a refugee! I hate that word. I *hate* it!'

Her hand slipped down and grasped my shoulder.

'Come to Dubai with us! Baba will pay. He'll get you into a good school. You don't have to stay here and sacrifice yourself like this.'

For a moment the idea floated gloriously in front of me, an iridescent bubble of hope. Then I shook her hand off.

'How could I leave Baba? He needs me. They all need me. It's not just the cooking and cleaning and all that.' I was struggling to find words, not even knowing what I was trying to say.

'I'm – I'm at the heart of this family,' I went on at last. 'I make this horrible tent into something like a home. Without me, Baba and Tariq and Malik would just sort of fall apart.'

Saba gave a shuddering sigh.

'No one needs me. Mama thinks she does, but she doesn't really. She – she *smothers* me. She's never let me do anything, for myself or for anyone else. You make me feel so small. Stupid. Pathetic. Like a – I don't know – like a baby.'

Babies. We'd been babies once, lying in our crib. She had cried, and had been picked up and carried away to a different life. I'd gone on sleeping, and become the person I was.

We heard Baba cough, and Uncle Hassan say irritably, 'It's so cold in here, Adnan. Your health alone is a reason for . . .'

'He's right, it's freezing,' whispered Saba. 'I don't know how you can bear it.'

'I'm used to it,' I said, trying not to sound arrogant.

'Well, anyway, you won't have to stand it much longer,' she said, yawning.

I was annoyed by her complacency.

'It's only January!' I snapped. 'It's ages till spring.'

'No, but you'll be in Amman by then.'

I jerked away from her, shocked.

'What? What are you talking about?'

'Didn't Baba Adnan tell you? No, he hasn't had a chance, has he?'

'Tell me what?'

'The plan. My Baba's plan.'

And then I suddenly knew what she was going to say. I suppose the idea had been in my mind from the beginning, but I'd forced it away.

'They discussed it all in the hospital,' she said, pulling me closer. 'I thought you knew. Baba needs a tenant for our flat in Amman. He wants you to take it. He'll get a place for you at my school. It's an international school, so you'll have to do catch-up classes in English.'

I could barely follow what she was saying. Her words bounced off me. I couldn't take them in.

'You could get Auntie Shirin to come and look after you, like she did in Damas—'

'Stop! Stop!' I wanted to put my hands over my ears to block out her voice. 'We couldn't possibly do all that. How could Baba ever afford the school fees in a fancy international school? How could we even manage to eat without Tariq's job? And Malik – he's sort of settled here. He can't move. Not just like that. Don't you understand anything, Saba? We have nothing! No money at all!'

She was silent for a moment, then she said humbly, 'I know, but I can't take in what it's like. I keep thinking, if I'd been you and you'd been me, and I'd had to manage like you have, I couldn't have done it. I'm so proud of you, Safiya. I just – I can't—'

And all of a sudden, she was the one who was crying.

There was a cough from beyond the partition, and Uncle Hassan called out, 'Are you girls all right in there?'

'Yes, we're fine!' we called back at exactly the same time, and Saba's tears hiccupped into weak laughter.

'He's totally fallen for you, you know,' she said. 'He's awestruck. He's going to give me a hard time making me live up to you. Once you're back at school, he'll want to know all your grades, and tick me off if mine aren't as good.'

I felt a chill settle over me and pulled away from her. The gulf between us had opened up again.

'I can't go back to school,' I said bitterly. 'There's no point in pretending. I'm a different person now. Anyway, Baba needs me to manage everything at home.'

'Well, I don't know about all that,' she said dismissively. 'It's what they're talking about now. They'll sort something out.' She gave another mighty yawn. 'I think we'd better try to go to sleep now, don't you?'

She curled into me and dropped off almost at once, but I gently pulled away and lay on my back, staring into the darkness. My mind was racing.

What was wrong with me? Why wasn't I overjoyed at the future that Saba had dangled in front of me? Did I really want to stay in this tent forever, freezing in the winter and frying in the summer? Did I want to spend the rest of my life cooking and washing and cleaning for three men, with crabby Aunt Zainab as my only female support, and dear old Abu Ali my one true friend?

There's always Perfumes of Paradise, I told myself.

I tried to warm myself again in the comfortable feeling of success and confidence that working for Um Khalid had given me. I couldn't.

I can't go back there, anyway, I thought. *There's no real job for me. Um Khalid replaced me as soon as she could. And, anyway, I really want to be a* doctor, *or a mathematician, or* design film sets. *I don't want to work in a beauty salon for the rest of my life.*

I thought I'd buried my old ambitions, but here they were, climbing out of their hiding place. Perhaps, if Uncle Hassan's plan went ahead, and he paid the fees at the expensive school, and I passed all my exams . . .

But it would never work! I told myself. *All these months I've longed to go back to school, but now it feels too late! How can I go back to giggling with other thirteen-year-old kids, being teased because of my teeth, having to put on a Jordanian accent all the time so they won't suspect that actually I'm a refugee? Anyway, Baba would never accept so much charity. And Auntie Shirin! She'd take over everything. Run the family. Do my work . . .*

In the main tent, I could hear Baba and Uncle Hassan moving about, ready to get into bed. I heard Baba say, 'What will you do, Malik, when we go to Amman?' and Malik answered, 'I'll stay in Azraq and bring my mother over from Syria. I'll ask Abu Fares if we can stay here in the tent until I earn enough to rent a proper flat.'

At last they settled down to sleep.

There was a deadness to the sounds of the night outside. The snow must have settled thickly. Beside me, Saba snuffled quietly in her sleep.

Then, just when I needed her, I heard my mother's voice.

Go on, she said. *Go on.*

I took a deep breath. A door was opening in front of me, beyond which lay an unknown road. Where would it lead? I couldn't know, but did I have the courage to take it? I would have to try. And, whether I did or not, would Saba and I ever truly find each other, as sisters and friends?

Perhaps, I thought. *Perhaps to everything. Yes.*

I turned over, fitting my back into Saba's curved body.

Go on, whispered Mama again. *Go on.*

'I will,' I said. 'I will.'

And finally I fell asleep.

A LETTER FROM THE AUTHOR

I hope you've enjoyed reading *A House Without Walls*. It's the story of one girl and her family, but it could be the story of any of the millions of people who have had to escape from Syria in recent years, fleeing from the murderous chaos that's destroyed their country. People of all ages have made the dangerous journey: grandparents and schoolchildren, fathers, mothers and babies, students, farmers, doctors, labourers, businessmen and every other kind of person you can think of.

Jordan is a beautiful country. Out in the countryside, olive trees march in lines up the hillsides, and villages made of cream-coloured stone top the crests. There are ancient ruins from Roman times which tourists from all over the world come to visit. But the region in the east where the refugees first find themselves, is harsh desert country. It's here that Syria and Jordan meet, and it was here where Safiya found herself, after the family's terrifying night journey from Damascus.

Last time I was in that part of the country it was September. In Azraq, a small town in what had once been a lush oasis, the intense heat of summer was softening. Wind blew grit and dust from the bare, flat earth into my eyes. In a few months' time, storms of driving rain would sweep across the desert, to be followed by ice and deep snow.

Many of those who have escaped from Syria and Iraq have passed through Azraq. Some have moved on into other parts of Jordan, looking for places where they can settle, perhaps hoping to join relatives or friends who might give them a helping hand. One in five find themselves in one of the vast, sprawling refugee camps, where they could be marooned for years until all hope has gone. Some stay in and around Azraq, making new homes from temporary shacks or tents, like Safiya and her family have to do. Others manage to scrape enough money together to rent a small flat or house.

I was warmly welcomed in Azraq. The teachers in a new community school were happy to show me their classrooms and books. The children threw their arms round me. When classes were over for the day, I went with them on the bus that dropped them off after school and watched them as they ran across the bare, stony ground towards the corrugated iron and thorn fences that surrounded their homes.

In one such home, I was given tea and cakes. As we sat on the cushions that lined the walls, a young girl showed me the beads she'd been given to thread into bracelets and necklaces. She would be selling them later to help pay for the family's food and clothes. I thought of her sometimes when I was writing the novel. Her education had been cut short, like Safiya's was.

It's very hard for people who have lost everything to accept what's happened to them. The struggle to make ends meet is really tough. When the war in Syria began, big aid agencies did a lot to help, but there are new conflicts now in other parts of the world, and budgets have been cut. In any case, they don't always find the people who need the help most.

Some small, local charities, working through a network of Jordanian helpers on the ground, are doing what they can. One of them, *Helping Refugees in Jordan*, gives food boxes every month to the hardest-hit families, as well as blankets and warm clothing in the winter months. This support can literally make the difference between life and death.

Helping Refugees in Jordan has linked up with a small charity, the Mandala Trust, to make it easy for people in the UK to help. For more information on the work that they do, visit their website **www.mandalatrust.org** or my own, **www.elizabethlaird.co.uk**

ACKNOWLEDGEMENTS

Many people helped me to write this book. In Jordan, I was looked after by Maher Atalef and Julie Delaire, who put me up in their flat in Amman and answered all my questions. Thank you so much, Maher and Julie!

While I was in Amman, Dr Rafat Bassam told me about the bottling plant he'd worked in after school and all weekend for years and years, to help support his family. He worked so hard that he was able to go right through medical school and become a doctor. Thank you, Dr Rafat, for giving me so many ideas. It was Jacki Scott of Hands on Hope who introduced me to Dr Rafat and told me about the many Syrian families she has helped, so thanks for that, Jacki, too.

In Azraq I was shown round by Israa Al-Shishani, who told me about the school she directs and the children she teaches. She took me to meet Abdul Aziz and his family, who had fled from Syria and are trying to make new lives in Jordan.

Catherine Ashcroft of Helping Refugees in Jordan has been an essential supporter and adviser. She was never too busy to answer my many calls and hundreds of questions and gave me lots of ideas. Her colleague Lexi Shereshewsky of the Syria Fund knows Azraq well. She suggested the name Perfumes of Paradise for the beauty salon, so thank you for that, Lexi!

Back in England, I couldn't even have got started without the support of everyone at Macmillan, especially Lucy Pearse my editor. She had a hard job pulling my chaotic first drafts into shape and put in a huge amount of work. Without her, this novel would never have seen the light of day.

Lucy Eldridge, the artist who did the lovely drawings, has added so much to the book. Your work is beautiful, Lucy, and I can't thank you enough for it.

Dr Marwa Mouazen of Edinburgh University has been a wonderful friend and adviser. She read through the whole manuscript, corrected my few bits of shaky Arabic and saved me from making embarrassing mistakes. She cooks great Syrian food too! Thank you for all that, Marwa.

Jane Fior has been my friend and mentor forever. She picked me up when I nearly foundered in the middle of the writing process and gave me the push I needed to go on. Thank you, as always, Jane.

ABOUT THE AUTHOR

Elizabeth Laird is the author of dozens of much-loved children's books, including *The Garbage King*, *The Fastest Boy in the World*, *Oranges in No Man's Land* and the UKLA award-winning *Welcome to Nowhere*. She has been shortlisted for the prestigious CILIP Carnegie Medal six times.

Elizabeth has lived in different countries in the Middle East and Africa and now lives in Britain, but she still likes to travel as much as she can. She has worked in Syrian refugee camps in Jordan, and twice visited Amman and Azraq, where *A House Without Walls* takes place.

'Sings with truth' *The Times*

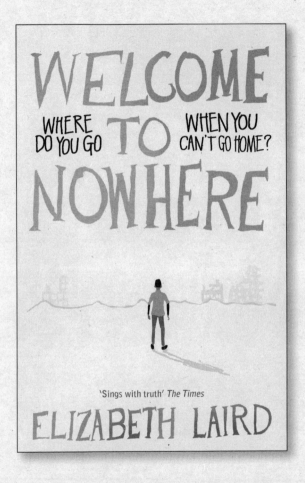

Forced to flee his home in Syria, Omar and his family face the dangers of civil war. A moving story of conflict and hope, winner of the UKLA Book Award.

'A tribute to the human spirit'
Times Educational Supplement

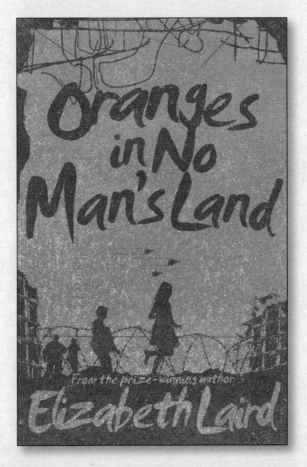

The gripping story of a ten-year-old girl who risks death
to make a life-saving dash through war-torn Beirut.

'A beautiful, important, heartfelt book'
Lauren St John, author of
The White Giraffe series

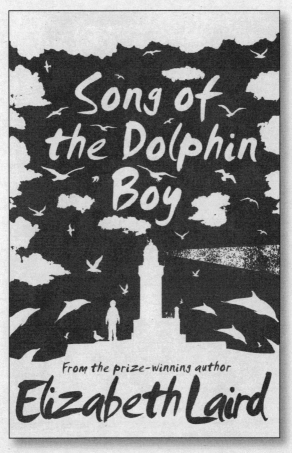

A powerful story about the importance of ocean
conservation and looking after your environment from
the award-winning author, Elizabeth Laird.